"You mustn't keep doing things for me."

Zoe tried to sound severe. "How will I ever pay you back?"

"Oh, I'm sure I'll think of something," Foster drawled, and his dark eyes seemed to twinkle with amusement. For a long time she seemed unable to drag her eyes away from his, then, smiling, she stood on tiptoe and pressed a kiss to his chin.

"You missed," he said softly, pointing solemnly to his mouth.

"What?" she asked blankly. Then realizing what he meant, she smiled again, and this time pressed a warm kiss on his mouth. It should have been brief, a mere peck, only somehow it didn't turn out that way. Staring dazedly at him, as though she couldn't understand what had happened, she backed away toward the stairs and positively scampered up them.

Emma Richmond says she's amiable, undomesticated and an incurable romantic. And, she adds, she has a very forbearing husband, three daughters and a dog of uncertain breed. They live in Kent. A great variety of jobs filled her earlier working years and, more recently, she's been secretary to the chairman of a group of companies. Now she devotes her entire day to writing, although she hasn't yet dispelled her family's illusions that she's reverting to the role of housekeeper and cook! Emma finds writing obsessive, time-consuming—and totally necessary to her well-being.

THE GENTLE TRAP

Emma Richmond

Harlequin Books

TORONTO • NEW YORK • LONDON
AMSTERDAM • PARIS • SYDNEY • HAMBURG
STOCKHOLM • ATHENS • TOKYO • MILAN

Original hardcover edition published in 1990
by Mills & Boon Limited

ISBN 0-373-17080-7

Harlequin Romance first edition February 1991

THE GENTLE TRAP

Printed in U.S.A.

CHAPTER ONE

SHE could recall the sequence of events with total clarity. She knew what had happened, could go over and over it in her mind and understand perfectly. Sitting on the hard upright chair by the window that gave a perfectly adequate, if not inspiring, view of the High Street, she watched with blank eyes the normal, everyday happenings of people shopping, talking, gossiping. What she couldn't see was her shop. Or what was left of her shop. *See*, she told her subconscious, so you do know. You do understand. And she gave a little smile, as though proud of her comprehension.

Zoe had been sitting in that same hard chair for the past nine hours, ever since, in fact, Meg Jessop, landlady of the Red Lion, where she was presently accommodated, had taken her by the arm and forcibly escorted her to this room. Meg Jessop presumably thought her still tucked up in bed, and Zoe smiled again. She had stayed tucked up in bed for precisely the length of time it had taken Meg Jessop to tuck her in, give her a glass of warm milk—which Zoe suspected contained aspirin—tiptoe out and close the door. The glass of milk now had a very nasty-looking skin on top. Zoe also knew she was cold, but doing something about it required more effort than she was able to summon up. Likewise the sudden rap on the door. She heard it, of course she heard it; there was nothing whatever the matter with her hearing. She also knew that a response was required—the fact that she felt unable to summon up the energy to call 'Come in' didn't at all alter the fact that she understood.

The door opened, and she turned her head. There was something vaguely familiar about the man who stood in the open doorway. With the part of her mind that was functioning normally, she knew that she knew him. Or had met him. She didn't examine her memory to find out how she knew him, or even what his name was; it seemed sufficient at the moment just to know that she knew him. He was tall and broad, and his thick dark hair was sprinkled with grey—Zoe frowned for a moment because she didn't quite remember that his hair had been grey before. His eyes were brown, a very dark brown—and, yes, those she remembered. She remembered that they never smiled—and his face, she remembered his face, an uncompromising sort of face, a determined chin, a firm mouth.

'Hello, Tiger,' he said softly.

Tiger? She examined the word, frowned, and a spark of memory stirred. Yes, Tiger. That was right. It was his name for her—a long time ago name, and her mouth curved in a small smile. A long, long time ago name. When she was seven. Zoe's beautiful dark blue eyes registered surprise, then pleasure. 'Foster,' she whispered.

Nodding, he closed the door very quietly behind him and walked across to stand in front of her, his hands loose by his sides.

'I once said,' he murmured quietly, 'that if ever you needed help, you were to ask me. Didn't I? Whatever you might need, if it were in my power to grant it, I would do so. This is something I can do. Do you understand?'

'Yes,' she whispered again, her voice a mere breath of sound.

'Good. Do you have any clothes? Belongings?'

'No, at least I don't think so, or only the things I was wearing,' and the stark truth of her statement finally brought the truth home to her. With the knowledge came a kind of acceptance. Glancing down at the nightclothes she was wearing, her eyes lightened fractionally. 'The pyjamas are courtesy of Meg.'

'Meg has appalling taste,' he commented in a very dry voice, and she gave a grunt of reluctant amusement.

'Yes, she has, but she's kind.'

'Mm. Can you dress yourself?'

'Yes, Foster,' she said with a delightfully wry smile that banished the shadows from her eyes. 'I'm not incapable.'

'Then get dressed,' he commanded. 'Now. I'll wait outside the door. All right?'

Nodding, Zoe made a little shooing motion with her hands. When he'd gone, she got reluctantly to her feet, not totally sure she believed that he'd been there, that it was him. Foster. Shaking her head in bemusement, she stripped off the pyjamas and dressed in the underwear that Meg had washed out for her, before pulling on her jeans and sweater.

When he returned, she was standing beside the bed, rather like a doll that someone had long since lost the key to. Walking across to her, he put a gentle finger beneath her chin and tilted her head up so that he could look down into her eyes. With a small, almost intimate smile, he slid his arm round her shoulders and led her out and downstairs to the lobby. Meg Jessop was standing by the heavy oak desk that served as the reception counter, her plain, homely face creased into lines of worry.

'Will she be all right?' she asked.

'Yes,' he said. Just that, no elaboration, no explanation, just yes, and another memory of him popped into Zoe's mind. She did remember that he had been a man of few words.

Taking a small white card from his pocket, he handed it to Meg. 'If you need to get in touch, call me.' Then, with nothing further to say, he propelled Zoe outside and into the car park, and she barely had time to squeeze Meg's hand in silent thanks. He opened the door of a dark red car, put her into the passenger seat and fastened her seatbelt. There were one or two people about, and they stared at her, but it didn't matter, not really, and then Foster was beside her, and they were moving out into the

High Street, and to the left. He had to go left because the road to the right was still cordoned off. There was tape across it to prevent people from walking that way—because of what had happened. With a funny little shiver Zoe wrapped her arms round herself, and leaned her head back.

'Where are we going?' she asked quietly.

'Home.'

Home: well, that had a nice comforting ring to it, she thought tiredly. Turning her head, she allowed her gaze to drift over him. Solid, dependable, attractive. Foster. Unbelievable. As though aware of her glance, he turned his head, and beautiful dark eyes made a brief assessment, and then, as though reassured by what he saw, he returned his attention to the road. Neither of them felt that there was any need for conversation.

They passed through towns, villages, came to a crossroads, turned left, and then they were driving between high, thick hedges and along a gravel drive, and the car came to a halt. It seemed very silent when the engine was turned off; Zoe's sigh sounded over-loud.

Gravel crunched noisily under their feet as they crossed to the open front door, and towards the lady with white hair who was waiting, looked worried, as worried as Meg Jessop. She seemed to be a housekeeper, and Zoe smiled vaguely at her, before being urged inside to the sitting-room and the welcome warmth of the roaring fire.

At Foster's bidding, she sat in the comfortable armchair that enveloped her slim five-foot-six frame and emphasised her look of frailty. The navy-patterned material seemed to whiten her face still further, to make her dark blue eyes look as black as her hair, which curled untidily across her shoulders. Staring at the fire that licked and curled round the logs, nibbled hungrily at the coal, Zoe saw another fire, heard the whoosh of flames as petrol ignited, the crackle and roar of wood burning, of masonry crashing to the ground, smelt the sickening stench of fumes and smoke, heard cries and sirens, orders shouted, ignored, obeyed—and, for the first time since it had happened, she began to cry. Not noisily, not in hurt or anger or disbelief, just allowed tears to trickle down her white face and drip from her chin to her sweater. She didn't attempt to stop them or wipe them away, just let them fall.

Turning her head on the soft cushion, she stared at the man sitting a few feet away in an armchair beside the fire. He was watching her, his face still, and she gave a wan smile, then a sniff, then finally wiped her palms across her wet cheeks. 'Hello.'

'Hello, Tiger,' he said softly. Picking up a box of tissues from the small table beside him, he passed it across.

She gave her nose a good blow, and relaxed back into the cushions again, her eyes still fixed on his face. 'Did you go to look?'

'Yes.'

'All gone?' she asked quietly.

'I'm afraid so,' he confirmed.

'Yes, that's what I thought.' With a long, shuddering sigh, she moved her gaze to the fire. 'Obviously meant not to be,' she added, with a rather lame attempt to be philosophical.

'No.'

She smiled then, a more natural smile, and moved her eyes back to his face. 'No,' she echoed. 'Never did use platitudes, did you? Always blunt, honest... Thank you,' she said softly.

'I owed you,' he said, equally softly, and just for a moment it looked as though he might smile. 'It was insured?'

'Yes.'

'Buildings and stock?'

'Yes... Foster! The tanker driver? He was killed?' When he nodded, she sighed again. 'I knew, really, just didn't want to admit it to myself. There was no way he could have survived that inferno. How did you know about me, about the fire?'

'It was on the news last night. Pictures of the fire, the fire-engines, police—and Zoe Mitchell standing like a little ghost, watching her home burn.'

'Two years,' she murmured, with a half-laugh that wasn't a laugh at all. 'Two years of hard work, decorating, fitting workstations, installing computers. Two years of hassle, beginning to grow, make money, and for what? They warned me about competition, about bank managers, about a fickle market—no one warned me about petrol tankers skidding on a wet road. No one warned me that that bend was dangerous... No one else was hurt?'

'No.'

'Well, at least that's something to be thankful for. And if I hadn't gone out to post a letter... Look on the bright side, hm?— Pick myself up, dust myself off,' and, just for a moment, her voice broke before she forced it back under control. 'Start all over again.'

'Not there, I'm afraid,' he said. 'From what I saw, not only the remains of your shop, but the one next to it will have to be demolished— and what the insurance company will have to say about that, we'll have to see. But right at this moment you need food, then sleep. Tomorrow is soon enough to make decisions.'

'I suppose so... Funny you should remember me after all these years.'

'You remembered me,' he pointed out gently.

'Yes. I did, didn't I? Such a long time ago,' Zoe said softly, returning her gaze to the fire. But then she'd had a photograph of him that she had looked at often. Had wondered about. Had he also had a photograph of her? 'Almost twenty years,' she murmured absently. 'You haven't changed much. A bit bigger than I remembered, hair going grey, your voice still soft, neutral, as though you never want anyone to know what you're thinking or feeling... And obviously I haven't changed much, either. Bit of a facer, that.' She smiled. 'I was rather a pudding...'

'Not a pudding now,' he murmured, his face almost smiling again. 'And maybe I wouldn't have known it was you, if you'd changed your name. Yet the eyes are the same deep blue, the hair still black as night...'

'Witch's hair,' she reflected, smiling at him. 'Remember?'

'Yes. I remember.' Shifting his position, he pushed a hand into his trouser pocket, and pulled out some notes. Peeling off two tens, he handed them to her, his eyes amused. 'Were you charging interest?' he asked, his fingers hovering over another ten-pound note.

Shaking her head, she took the two tens, her eyes distant as she remembered that long ago day when she had emptied her piggy-bank, had given him all her savings. 'Nineteen pounds, eight shillings and sixpence-halfpenny,' she murmured. 'It was a fortune then, wasn't it? Twenty pounds? I don't have any change.' She smiled sadly, as she realised she didn't have any anything.

'Did you ever get the bike you were saving up for?'

'No, I never did.' Then, with a small impish smile, she admitted, 'I wasn't allowed to have one. As punishment for breaking open my piggy-bank and spending all my money. And then, to compound my wilfulness, as they called it, not telling them what I'd spent it on. But I couldn't do that, could I? It was a secret.'

'A big secret to expect a seven-year-old to keep,' he murmured, with his fascinating half-smile that was beginning to intrigue her. 'I often wondered over the years whether you'd been punished—it troubled me that you might have been.'

'A smack,' she smiled, 'and sent to bed without any tea. A few rows, arguments, the third degree. Watched like a hawk for a while, and any birthday money I got after that went straight into a Post Office savings account! Fast as you like! Odd that they never connected your disappearance with my missing savings. My mother mentioned it not so long ago, when she was over from the States—Dad died ten years ago, she married an American, lives in Ohio now,' she explained quickly. 'One of her grandchildren, step-grandchildren, I suppose, had a piggy-bank very much like mine, and it reminded her.'

'Did you tell her?'

'No. I don't know why. Once a secret, always a secret, maybe. She said I was stubborn.'

'And wilful. Determined. And my very good friend.'

'Yes. An unlikely alliance, wasn't it? A tough, moody fifteen-year-old boy and a pugnacious little girl of seven. Tiger and Foster,' she recalled with a soft reminiscent smile. 'I scratched that on my desk at school. It was a long time after you left that I discovered that your name wasn't Foster. I kept a photograph of you—did you know that? I asked my mother one day if she remembered you, knew what had happened to you. Foster, I said. His name was Foster. She was absolutely horrified. Told me that I was wicked, until I explained. Did you mind it so very much?'

'Not from you,' he said, his voice as always soft, hypnotic.

'But the others? Children can be very cruel, can't they? But I used to hear them shouting Foster after you, and, naturally enough, I thought it was your name. I didn't know that you'd been fostered. Probably wouldn't even have known what it meant.'

Leaning comfortably back in the chair, he suddenly chuckled, an infectious little sound that captivated Zoe. 'How could I mind it when you were always so determined to right all my wrongs? It was such an odd feeling, to know that, out of the whole wide world, the only person who cared about me was a little girl with short chubby legs, who would march defiantly into the fray and defend me. I can see you now, your face set in a scowl as you ticked off all the bully-boys. Wasn't at all good for my image, you know, to have you tagging my every step. I thought myself very grown-up, and well able to take care of myself.'

'Well, I expect you could. I seem to remember some of the boys sporting black eyes from time to time. Yet you were never unkind to me, never told me to push off, as the others did.'

'Just as well. You wouldn't have given me your savings if I had, would you?' With another of his fascinating smiles, he got up. 'Come and have something to eat.'

Standing in front of her, he held his hand out, and when Zoe had put her own into it he pulled her up to stand before him. The top of her head barely touched his chin, and, her hand still held in his, she stared up into his face. A strong, hard face, without expression, yet she had never felt intimidated by him. Nor did she now.

'I'm sorry,' she apologised softly. 'I've been rambling on, haven't I? So I wouldn't have to think about the fire and everything.'

'I know.'

Yes, this man would always know, and the thought was somehow comforting.

Zoe managed to eat a little of the soup which his housekeeper put before her, and a few mouthfuls of the steak and kidney pie, but only because she thought the housekeeper might be upset if she didn't eat anything. She wasn't really very hungry. There was a sick, empty feeling inside her, and, as she gazed sightlessly at her plate, her eyes filled with tears. With a sudden, wretched little movement, she laid down her knife and fork, and covered her eyes. 'I'm sorry,' she whispered, 'I . . .'

Getting swiftly to his feet, Foster walked round the table and squatted beside her chair. His large hands gripped hers hard, before he said softly, 'Look at me, Zoe.' When she turned her head and stared miserably down at his face, he continued, 'You have no need to apologise to me, ever. You've lost your home, your business—all the memories of twenty-six years of living. Did you think I expected you to be bright? A riveting companion?'

Shaking her head, a weak smile pulling at her trembling mouth, she whispered, 'No, but, oh, Foster, I can't believe that it's all gone. I worked so hard, was so proud of my little flat, my pictures...'

'Oh, darling, don't.' Standing, he pulled her up into his arms, and held her tight in a comforting grip that she didn't want to break.

'I'm behaving like a baby,' she muttered against his strong chest, liking the feel of him, wanting to burrow closer.

'No, you're behaving like a lady who's exhausted, and who has had too much to bear on her own.' Taking her by surprise, he swung her up into his arms. Smiling gently down at her woebegone face, he said softly, 'Bed.'

Carrying her out and up the stairs, he called for his housekeeper. Walking along the landing, he carried her into one of the bedrooms, then sat her on the edge of the bed. 'Laura will help you into bed, and then I'll come back. All right?'

'Yes. Thank you... Foster?' and, when he turned back, she added softly, 'I'm glad it was you.'

'Yes. So am I.'

As Laura came in, her kind face creased in lines of concern, Zoe summoned up another smile. 'Sorry I'm being such a pest.'

'And I'm sorry I can't make it all better. Come on, into bed with you. I've put out one of my nighties—it is clean,' she added, awkwardly.

'Oh, Laura,' Zoe gulped, brief amusement overshadowing her misery, 'I'm sure it is.'

'It's difficult, isn't it? When people are strangers. No knowing what to do for the best. But I am sorry, love, and if there's anything I can do, you only have to ask.'

'Thank you.' Climbing between the sheets, Zoe stared at Laura, who was folding her discarded clothes. 'Have you known Foster long?' she asked curiously.

'Foster,' the housekeeper echoed with a small smile. 'I haven't heard him called that before.'

'No. It was a name I gave him when I was a little girl.'

'Ah, that explains it, then. I guessed you must be old friends. He was that distressed when we saw the newsflash.'

'Was he? How could you tell?' she asked teasingly, with another smile, and Laura laughed.

'He goes even more still, if you know what I mean,' she explained, her brow furrowed in thought. 'Sort of controlled. It's hard to explain, really—he doesn't give very much away. But I like working for him. Always know where you are with him. He never says things he doesn't mean. Blunt, and that suits me just fine. I'm a bit that way myself. Now, do you want anything? A nice cup of tea?'

'No, thank you, Laura. You've been very kind. I'm sorry if I've put you to a lot of trouble.'

'I may have white hair, young lady, but that doesn't mean I'm on my last legs. In point of fact, I've had white hair since I was thirty. Shock, they think it was, when my husband died.'

'I didn't mean to imply...'

'Bless you, I know you didn't. But for the record, I'm fifty-seven, still a bit of life left in the old girl yet. Now, you snuggle down and get some sleep. Things always look better after a good night's rest.' With a last smile, she bustled out and Zoe heard her say something to Foster, who was presumably waiting on the landing.

He came in a few minutes later, and perched on the edge of the bed. Picking up her hand, he held it for a moment as he stared down at her.

'All right? Warm enough?'

'Yes.'

'Good.' Tucking her hand beneath the covers, he gave her a small smile. 'Get some sleep. Don't think about it, consider it, worry about it. Easier said than done, I know, but try, hm? We'll sort things out tomorrow.'

'Yes,' she agreed softly, 'but I'm still trying to absorb the fact that I'm actually here with you. So many years—funny how things turn out, isn't it?'

'Hysterical,' he murmured with his funny half-smile.

'Oh, you, you know what I mean!'

'Yes, I know what you mean.' Putting out his hand, he pushed her tumbled hair off her face, then rubbed his thumb gently down her cheek in a soothing, comforting gesture, his expression, as always, unfathomable. 'Did you grow out of falling over every five minutes?'

With a little laugh, she nodded. 'Always in the wars, wasn't I? But then my friend Foster always seemed to be on hand to pull me up and dust me off. Remember when I fell in the stinging nettles?'

'Oh, yes.'

'Practically exhausted the whole of the South-East's supply of dock leaves and went home looking like the Jolly Green Giant. My mother was horrified.'

'I also remember when you fell in the newt pond—and I got the blame for pushing you in. Come on, close your eyes, we can talk tomorrow.'

Nodding, she obediently closed her eyes, then snapped them open again. 'Foster?'

'Mm?'

'Thank you.'

'Pleasure. Go to sleep.'

'Yes. Goodnight.'

Surprisingly, she fell asleep almost straight away, and when Foster looked in half an hour later she was curled up on her side, her hand beneath her cheek like a little girl, her dark lashes damp and spiky from her tears.

It was gone ten when she woke the next morning. Foster was sitting on the end of her bed dressed in jeans and an Aran sweater, a mug of tea clasped in his large hands, his dark eyes steadily on hers. Gazing at him, as she remembered all that had happened, all his kindness, she smiled. 'Good morning.'

Giving an amused little nod—at least she thought it was amused, but it wasn't very easy to tell—he asked, 'Feeling better?'

'Yes. Much.' Zoe wasn't sure that she did. Wasn't sure of anything very much, and his being there when she woke didn't give her time to think now. Which was presumably why he had done it. Hoisting herself up on the pillows, she hitched Laura's voluminous nightdress on to her shoulder. The housekeeper was about a size eighteen. Zoe was a size ten, and she smiled ruefully.

She felt neither embarrassed nor awkward. It seemed right that she should be here. Odd, that, that she felt so comfortable with Foster, and that she had recognised him after so many years. Yet he hadn't really changed that much. He'd always been tall, even at fifteen, but gangling then. Now he was solid muscle and warm tanned flesh, and she thought that he was probably one of the most attractive men she'd seen in a long time. Yet, even if he had changed, she thought that she would always have recognised his eyes. So deep and dark that the brown looked almost black, and those thick lashes that were most definitely wasted on a man. Tipping her head on one side, she examined him in the light streaming through the window. Such a strong, controlled face, impossible to read.

There was a faint, humorous light in his eyes as Zoe continued to examine him, and she grinned, the trauma of yesterday beginning to fade. 'Sorry, I didn't mean to stare,' she said. 'I just find it so hard to believe that I'm really here, with you.' Then, indicating the mug he still held, she asked teasingly, 'Is that for me?' and when he nodded and handed it across she accepted it gratefully, curling her palms round the warm china. 'Thank you. What happens now?'

'You stay here. Get your life back together. You'll need to speak to the insurance company, the building society...'

'No, that at least is something I won't have to do. I didn't have it on a mortgage—Mum left me her house over here when she moved to the States, and I used the proceeds from the sale to buy the shop.'

'But there are still the police, friends, relatives, whatever, and you'll need to go to the bank, buy some clothes.'

'Mm. The bank manager will be pleased, won't he?' she mumbled, a shadow moving in her lovely eyes. 'I have an enormous overdraft. Best find a job, try and pay some of it off. I don't suppose the insurance company will settle very quickly, do you?'

'No.'

Making a determined effort to push back the despair that threatened to swamp her, she asked, 'Where exactly are we?'

'Not far from Petworth; the town is about five miles away from the house. Don't worry about it.'

'No. Not much point, is there? Worrying won't solve my problems.' Fine words, brave words, and she gave a humourless smile; yet it was true. What can't be cured must be endured. Sound advice; better start following it, she thought, sipping absently at her tea, else she'd turn into one of those dreadful people who were always harping on about their misfortunes. 'I'll finish my tea, then get up,' she added, with a determined smile.

'Fine.' Getting to his feet, Foster indicated the door to her right. 'Bathroom's through there. Get washed, dressed, come and have some breakfast, then we'll go into town and make a start.'

'All right, and thank you for being so—well—nice,' she added, with a deprecating shrug when she couldn't think of a better word. 'It's lovely to meet you again, know you're well ... You are well?'

'Oh, yes,' he murmured, with the almost-
smile again. 'And perhaps I ought just to
mention,' he added, his eyes creased with
humour, 'that your nightie just fell off.'
Turning on his heel, he walked out. 'Five
minutes!' he called over his shoulder, as Zoe
hastily dragged the nightie back into position,
her face pink.

'Voyeur!' she yelled after him, then gave a
snort of amusement. Fell off, indeed! She
doubted that she'd ever been in it. Finishing
her tea, she wasted most of the five minutes
thinking about him. David Campbell, her
mother had said his name was. Foster. And it
had taken a fire and the loss of her home to
bring them together again. Sighing, she threw
back the covers and headed for the bathroom.

The image reflected in the full-length mirror
opposite the door made her halt in shock. God,
she looked like the wreck of the Hesperus. Her
hair, unruly at the best of times, now looked
like a tangled hedge. And the nightie most
definitely revealed more than it covered. It
sagged and hung in unattractive folds, the low
neckline coming way below her own not very
ample bust, and she burst out laughing. Lord,
what an impression to make on an old friend!
Shaking her head at herself, she walked across
to the shower.

Emerging a few minutes later, wrapped in a
towel, she noted the new toothbrush in the
rack, the new hairbrush still in its cellophane
wrapper on the shelf over the sink, and she

smiled again. It was almost as though she'd been expected. A hairdrier sat on the vanity unit, a jar of moisturiser and cleanser, a packet of cottonwool. Or was it that he was used to female guests staying unexpectedly? she wondered thoughtfully. Foster was a very attractive man—and for twenty years he'd been a yardstick by which she had measured other men, and found them wanting. Crazy. The fact that he'd been her hero when she was seven didn't at all mean that he would be one to her at twenty-six.

Yet she didn't want to be disillusioned, didn't want the dream to die. Neither did she like the idea of other women sharing his life, and her hand froze midway as it reached for the moisturiser, while she considered that very odd thought. It shouldn't matter a damn to her who shared his life—yet, inexplicably, it did.

CHAPTER TWO

FOSTER was leaning against the wall at the bottom of the stairs when Zoe came down, and she smiled. Glancing at the grandfather clock beside him, she saw that she'd been fifteen minutes. 'Only ten minutes late,' she murmured.

'Mm.' Straightening, he held his hand out to her. 'Before we have breakfast, you'd better come and meet the Major.'

'The Major?' she echoed, puzzled, then smiled as he tugged her towards the kitchen and pushed open the door. A large German Shepherd dog sat facing them, and Zoe was reminded of the children's story of the tinderbox, and the large dog that guarded the gold. At a sign from Foster he padded forward and Zoe held her hand out to be sniffed. 'He's lovely,' she exclaimed, scratching behind his ears.

'He's a guard dog,' Foster corrected drily.

'But you love him anyway,' she teased, giving him a warm smile.

'Come and have some breakfast.' With a little shake of his head, he took her elbow and led her into the room where they'd eaten dinner the night before, and Zoe glanced round curiously. She hadn't really been in any fit state to notice her surroundings the day before. Wide windows overlooked the garden and the woods beyond. There was a bird table on the lawn, and sparrows and a blackbird were fighting for the food that had obviously just been put out. A pale sun threw light and spurious warmth across the table that was set for two. The curtains at the window beside her, and those at the french doors, were a heavy Sanderson print, the carpet pale green, the walls cream. An airy, peaceful room, not the sort of room she would have expected Foster to have. Then she smiled to herself, because she didn't really know what sort of room she'd thought he would have. Unaware of the expressions flitting across her exquisite face, she turned to smile at Laura as she brought in the breakfast.

She was hungry, she found, and ate every scrap of the eggs and bacon, two slices of toast and marmalade, earning herself an approving nod from the housekeeper. Nursing her coffee in her hands, she asked, 'Does Laura live in?'

'No. She has a little cottage not far from here. Like you, Laura values her independence. She's a widow.'

And was very glad of being able to work locally, Zoe mentally completed. Was he an easy man to work for? Generous? Tolerant? It was hard to know.

'Ready?' he asked. 'We have a lot to do this

morning.' And Foster wasn't a man to waste time, she thought, with an inward smile.

She'd never been to Petworth and she looked around her curiously as Foster found a place to park in Golden Square.

'You can explore later,' he murmured, as she lagged behind to look round her.

Giving a small acquiescent smile, she allowed herself to be led away, turning her thoughts to more urgent matters, like explaining her problems to a strange bank manager, arranging for an extended loan from her own branch. Her elbow was taken in a firm grip as Foster escorted her into the bank, and she was amused to notice the almost standing to attention of the clerks. No hanging about waiting to be noticed for Foster. No joining of queues. The line in front of the clerk nearest them was hastily abandoned, and in two seconds he was through the security door and in front of them.

'Mr Campbell, it's nice to see you again,' he exclaimed obsequiously, and Zoe suppressed a grin. 'How may we help?'

'Is Lester in?'

'Yes, of course. Perhaps you'd like to come through and I'll tell Mr Graham that you're here.' With a little bob of his head to Zoe, he led the way into the interior of the bank. If Mr Graham was the manager, would he too immediately abandon whatever he was doing in order to see Foster? she wondered.

'Did you make an appointment?' she asked softly, as the clerk went off to alert Lester.

'No,' he said, turning to give her an amused glance.

'I always have to,' she retorted, not altogether humorously.

'Yes. But then you aren't me. Are you?'

'No.' But what made him so special?

'Mr Graham will see you now,' the clerk murmured, rushing back to them, and then escorted them through into the manager's office where a tall, thin man was waiting. Only not as tall as Foster. Comparing him to the other man only emphasised Foster's impressive size and air of authority.

'David, it's good to see you again,' he greeted enthusiastically, with a small smile for Zoe. 'What can I do for you? Please sit down.'

'I want to make arrangements for Miss Mitchell to draw funds from my account...'

'Oh, Foster, no!' she exclaimed. 'I can't do that!'

Ignoring her, not even glancing at her, he continued smoothly, 'As from today.'

'Yes, of course, I'm sure we can arrange that. I'll need a specimen signature, a few forms,' he explained apologetically. 'If you'll excuse me for a moment, I'll go and get the necessary documentation.'

As soon as he was out of the room, Zoe turned on Foster. 'I can't let you do that!' she exclaimed crossly. 'God only knows when I'll be able to pay you back—apart from which, you know nothing about me. I could disappear and not pay you back, I could——'

'You could be quiet and stop being stupid,' he said quietly. 'You need money, I have money. Situation resolved. And I should be enormously grateful if you wouldn't take me to task in front of Lester.'

Staring at him in exasperation, noting the glint in his eye, she subsided with a little sniff. 'He's going to think . . .'

'I don't give a damn what he thinks. That isn't what he's paid for.'

Of course it wasn't. But that wouldn't stop him speculating, and it was rather arrogant of Foster to assume that his word was law; then she had to forcibly remind herself that she did not know him—did not know what his word was or wasn't. Knew virtually nothing about him at all. Recollections of him twenty years ago could be way off beam.

The formalities were completed in what seemed no time at all, and Zoe accompanied Foster from the bank in something of a daze, two hundred pounds tucked securely into her jeans pocket. 'Shall I meet you back here?' she asked meekly, as they stood outside on the pavement.

'Where were you thinking of going?' he asked smoothly, one eyebrow quirking upward.

'I thought I was going to get some clothes,' she murmured, confused.

'You are. But not here. We'll drive into Chichester—there's a better selection.'

'Yes, Foster,' she said obediently and he gave his half-smile again before urging her to get into the car.

'I'm glad to see you're learning.'

'Oh, I am, I am, only don't expect instant obedience all the time, will you?' she asked softly.

'No. Nor would I want it. But in some things...'

'You like to be top doggy, I know——'

'Men usually do, wasn't that what you were about to add?'

'Only mentally.' She smiled. 'I am grateful, Foster, don't think I'm not. It's just that...'

'You're not very good at accepting things...'

'No. I don't like being beholden to anyone. I'm sorry if I sounded less than gracious.'

'Apology accepted,' he murmured, with that half-smile she was beginning to watch for.

'It won't break the bank?' she asked tentatively.

'No. It won't break the bank.'

'No, that's what I figured. Judging by Mr Graham's manner, you are a very valued customer. You're rich, aren't you?'

'Yes, Zoe. I'm rich,' he confirmed, turning to glance at her.

'You always said you would be. One day, you said, by the time I'm twenty-five, I'll be a millionaire. How old were you?' she teased, because she didn't really believe he was a millionaire. Wealthy, yes. But not a millionaire.

'Twenty-two,' he said simply, and she looked at him in shock. He wasn't joking.

'My God!' she exclaimed softly. 'Runaway to millionaire in seven years, that must have taken some doing.'

'Yes. And all thanks to a chubby little witch who gave me her savings.'

'Oh, no, I can't flatter myself that I had anything to do with it. If I hadn't given you the money, you'd have found another way... Do you mind if I ask what you do?'

'I buy and sell, play the stock markets, shares, gilts. I buy and sell property, commodities. I buy something no one wants—create a market...'

'An entrepreneur, one might say?'

'One might easily say that,' he murmured. 'I'm very good at what I do.'

'Mm. The Midas touch.'

'Yes. It would seem so... and here we are in Chichester,' he said drily.

When they'd finished her shopping, they had lunch in a small restaurant, and Zoe watched him surreptitiously. Watched how he handled himself, how he handled other people; noted the warmth of his skin, the faint tan, the length of his dark lashes; and she wondered what facets of his character that bland face hid. Even when they'd finished and they left the restaurant, she continued to puzzle about him, which at least took her mind off her own troubles.

'Stop it,' he reproved softly, as he settled her in the car.

'Stop what?' she asked, confused.

'Speculating about me. Just take me as you see me.'

Nodding in a rather dazed way, she stared from the window as he drove them back to the house. He might just as well have told her to stop breathing; and to take him as she saw him could be dangerous, because she was beginning to think that she wasn't seeing him very well at all. As they drove in through the gates, she stared at the house curiously. It wasn't in the least pretentious. A square, solid sort of house built of grey stone. It didn't look in the least like the house of a millionaire. 'How much ground do you have?'

'Ten acres. Five are planted out with Christmas trees.'

'Christmas trees!' she exclaimed, with a smile. 'Is that a lucrative turnover?'

'Hopefully. Five pence a sapling, should sell for upwards of five pounds at maturity. Five-year turnaround. There was a nursery here once, and I might renew the licence if I can find someone to run it. I don't know yet.'

'How long have you been here?'

'I bought the house four years ago, lived in it for two.'

'Will you stay?'

'Maybe. Maybe not. Depends,' he said laconically.

With a rueful smile, she climbed out and hugged her new black leather jacket round her, a present from Foster, not out of the two hundred pounds.

'Make yourself at home, do whatever you have to do. I have to take the Major out for a walk. I'll be about an hour.'

'Could I take him?' she asked impulsively. 'I need—well, I . . .'

'Need some time on your own,' he put in gently. 'Yes, of course you do. Come on, I'll get you his lead.'

Zoe walked slowly, her thoughts muddled, as the Major ran off, chasing whatever it was that dogs chased. She had no worries that he wouldn't come back. Foster had trained him well. Foster, she thought with a sigh. She needed to think about Foster, and about staying with him while she sorted herself out. Leaning against a thick oak, she stared unseeingly at the grey sky glimpsed between the bare branches. What was she going to do? That was the question. Unfortunately, she didn't know the answer. Although it was beginning to occur to her that she could do as she wished: the slate was wiped clean. Could be, and do, whatever she wanted. A new beginning.

For as long as she could remember, people had dumped on her. Not in a nasty way, and mostly it was her own fault. She seemed to give off an aura of competence, or so people had told her. Someone who could cope, who always knew the answers. It wasn't true, of course, but that was what people thought. When her father had died, her mother had turned to her. Zoe would look after her, she'd said. And Zoe had. She had supported her through her grief, stayed in to keep her company, shelved her own plans until her mother had met Hank and moved to the States, leaving Zoe free to get on with her own life. Her own career.

Computer programming fascinated her, and she took course after course in the evenings, learning all she could. Analyst programmers were much in demand. Then she'd met Peter, had thought herself in love, become engaged to him. And Peter had dumped his problems on her. The problem of his mother and his job prospects—until she had grown tired of being the strong one. Tired, if she was totally honest, of pretending an affection she was no longer able to feel. She had broken off the engagement and moved to a small village in Buckinghamshire, for no better reason than because she had liked the look of the place when she'd driven through it one day.

With her savings, the residue of the money from her mother's house, which Zoe had sold when it became hers on her mother's departure, she bought a shop and the flat above it. Then she had started her own business dealing in computers, offering a consultancy service, programming. Despite all the odds, she had done well. She had also, for one reason or another, been loaded with the troubles of everyone in the village. With Sue's divorce, the Fords' baby-sitter, Meg Jessop's bunions. If people had a problem, they brought it to her. Or so it had seemed. Sometimes her shop resembled nothing more than a meeting of the WI. With a wry smile she admitted that, had she stayed after the fire, they all would have rallied round. Only, unlike them, she didn't like, or want, her troubles aired. She preferred to cope with them on her own.

So why had she allowed Foster to organise her life? Because she'd been in shock? Was still in shock? But, having allowed Foster to do so, might it not turn out for the best? Here she was not known. Here she could change. Do what she wanted with her life. Become selfish? Aloof? She could be friendly without allowing people to intrude, couldn't she? When the insurance money came through she could buy a small cottage. Not actually in a village, but, like Foster in his ten acres, near enough for company if she wanted it, far enough away to be left in peace. A policy of non-involvement— was that what she wanted? She didn't honestly know. Ah, well, as Foster said, take it one day at a time.

Calling the dog, she turned for home. Except that it wasn't her home, it was Foster's, and that was a fact that she would do well to remember. It would be far too easy to fall into the habit of leaning on him, and that would be foolish. So don't get to like him too much, Zoe, she warned herself.

When she got back to the house, her little Peugeot was sitting out in the drive, and she stared at it in disbelief. Rushing inside, she nearly knocked Foster flying, as he strode along the hall.

'Whoa!' he said humorously, catching hold of her in his strong hands. 'What's the rush?'

'My car's outside,' she exclaimed breathlessly.

'So I should hope; we aren't normally troubled by car thieves.'

'Foster! Don't be aggravating! Did you arrange it?'

'Of course,' he said mildly, a little smile playing round his mouth. 'You'll need a car down here.'

'That's not the point,' she muttered, trying to sound severe and failing. 'You mustn't keep doing things for me—how will I ever pay you back?'

'Oh, I'm sure I'll think of something,' Foster drawled, and his dark eyes seemed actually to twinkle with amusement, which thoroughly diverted Zoe for a moment. For a long while she seemed unable to drag her eyes away from his, then, with a wide smile, she stood on tiptoe and pressed a kiss to his chin.

'Thank you.'

His face serious, almost severe, apart from the dancing eyes, he pointed solemnly to his mouth. 'You missed,' he said softly.

'What?' she asked blankly. Then, realising what he meant, she smiled again, and this time pressed a warm kiss on his mouth—which should have been brief, a mere peck, only somehow it didn't quite turn out that way. Staring dazedly at him, as though she couldn't for the life of her understand what had happened, she backed away towards the stairs, her eyes still fixed bemusedly on his amused face. 'I have to take my muddy shoes off,' she mumbled, before turning tail and practically scampering up the stairs. Her mouth felt all tingly, and she put a hand up to touch her fingers to her bottom lip, then snatched it away, disgusted with herself for so over-reacting. Good lord, he must have thought she'd gone potty! It had only been a brief kiss, for goodness' sake! Yet it was odd how, for days afterwards, she could still almost feel it.

Time passed swiftly as she lazed around, doing very little. Laura waited on her, hand, foot and finger, and seemed more than happy to do so. But Zoe wasn't used to being waited on, and she began to get fidgety. What she really needed was something to do. Yet, despite the fact that Foster seemed busy in his study, he wouldn't let her help, merely told her to take it easy, amuse herself. Doing what, she wondered irritably?

She rang Meg, reassured her that she was all right. Rang one or two friends who might have seen the Press reports on the fire, and be worried. She rang the insurance company, to be told that a claim form was in the post, and then she rang the computer companies for whom she had been an agent, the clients to whom she had commitments, the VAT officials. They were very understanding: would she let them know when she was ready to set up again? She would, if she ever did. Because she still hadn't decided whether that was what she wanted to do. She wrote letters, filled in forms, so that she could get her driving licence, passport, cheque-book and credit cards replaced. She'd need new insurance documents for the car. MOT certificate. God, she thought despondently, so many things to replace.

That evening, she was also supposed to be making a list of all the other things she'd lost in the fire, only her mind wasn't very firmly on her task; it was on Foster, as it seemed to be so often now. It was beginning to trouble her, this constant preoccupation with him... Then Zoe gave a guilty start as he walked in.

'Hello, you're looking very solemn. Feeling neglected?'

'Neglected? Good heavens, no! I haven't expected you to entertain me, Foster.' Which she hadn't, not exactly, although she had to admit that she would have liked more of his company.

'Just as well, isn't it?' he asked wryly. 'But then neither did I intend to ignore you. One or two things came up that I've had to deal with. Beginning to feel restless?' he asked gently.

'No. Yes. Oh, I don't know. I'm beginning to feel a bit of a parasite, and every time I try to come up with some constructive ideas, my mind goes blank.'

'Then leave it blank. Let yourself drift. I don't imagine that there have been many occasions in your life when you've allowed yourself to do so. What were you writing?'

'Oh, trying to make a list of all I lost.' Then she gave a wry grimace as she stared down at the complicated doodles covering the pad. 'Not very constructive, I'm afraid,' she added, as he walked across and twitched it out of her hand.

'Not very, no. Like a drink? Whisky?'

'Mm, whisky's fine. Ice, if you have it.'

'Tut, tut, sacrilege.' Giving her a slight smile, he took the ice-bucket to the kitchen, and returned a few minutes later with it full. Handing her a drink, he sat in the armchair by the fire.

'So tell me about Zoe since the age of seven,' he murmured. 'Still casting spells?'

Laughing, not fully realising how much more alive she became when in his presence, she took a sip of her drink. 'I gave them up when I was about ten, I think. What a precocious little horror I was. Witch indeed.'

'Why did you always defend me?' he asked lazily.

Smiling faintly, Zoe stared down into her drink, before admitting slowly, 'I don't really know. I think I decided you were a sort of misunderstood hero. You always seemed to be getting beaten up by the other boys, and odds of five or six to one seemed grossly unfair—although what I thought I could do, standing in front of you with my arms protectively wide, I haven't the foggiest.' Watching Foster from the corner of her eye, she saw him smile and she added quietly, 'I overheard conversations sometimes between the adults. Poor boy, the Stevenses don't look after him properly, they'd say. Always looks hungry, ill-clothed, and I'm sure George Stevens beats him... Did he?' she asked softly.

'Sometimes; his leather belt. It was no more than I expected. Although I don't suppose all foster-parents beat their children! And I didn't exactly put myself out to develop winning ways. Did I?'

'No,' she murmured, aching for him, for the boy he had been. 'But then all the best heroes are silent, stoic, sullen. Aren't they?'

'Are they?' he asked, amused.

'Yes... What happened to your real parents?'

'I've no idea,' he said blandly, but Zoe wasn't sure that she believed him.

'You never tried to find them?'

'No. Why should I? Would you? If you'd been abandoned at the age of four? Dumped on the steps of the local orphanage? Then the long hassle with the social services trying to get her to take me back. She kept refusing. Would you?'

'No,' she said helplessly. 'Were you happy up until the age of four? Do you remember?'

'Oh, yes, I remember. Being beaten leaves an indelible mark, Zoe.'

'Your father?' she asked softly.

'Mm. It's not important. Tell me about you. Why have you never married? You're an astonishingly beautiful woman—there must have been men.'

'Oh, yes. Bees round a honeypot,' she murmured with a touch of cynicism.

'But?'

'Men don't like women to know best—and invariably I do. Or think I do,' she grinned. 'I'm impossibly arrogant, you know. Oh, they all spout nonsense about how they admire clever women—but not for them. Not to live with. Do they?'

'Don't they?'

'No. They like soft fluffy women who defer to them. Are dependent, flatter their egos—and maybe I would, if I ever found a man I could defer to, could respect. Or maybe not. I'm not very romantic, not very deferential. A pragmatist.'

'No,' he said softly. 'Wilful, a handful.'

'Mm. I hurt men's pride, you see,' she explained, her eyes full of teasing laughter. His face remained impossibly bland, but he was laughing inside, she could tell—and she wanted to make him laugh, she found, to tease him, flirt with him.

'Go on,' he prompted, when she continued to stare at him blankly.

'What? Oh.' Pulling herself together, she declared hastily, 'I was engaged once. Found a man who didn't mind me being bossy. Lasted about a month. He drove me insane. Kept wanting my advice, wanting me to solve his problems. How's that for perverse?' she murmured, with a little grin.

'Pretty much par for the course, I would imagine. Decided what you want to do?'

'No,' she admitted, with a little sigh.

'Then stay here. I find I quite enjoy having you around,' said Foster softly, his dark eyes intent on hers.

'Do you?'

'Yes. You may stay as long as you choose.'

'Then thank you.' Holding his gaze for a long moment, she had a sudden feeling of entrapment, then shook off the crazy thought. In truth, the thought of staying here with him was extraordinarily pleasing. 'Why have you never married?' she asked curiously. 'If I may return the compliment, you are an astonishingly attractive man.'

'Oh,' said Foster slowly, 'too lazy, I expect. Why? Want to take me on?'

'No,' she said hastily, without stopping to think, then gave a lame smile when he chuckled. 'I'm beginning to think you might be more than I could handle.' Especially after her stupid reaction to his kiss in the hall, she thought, feeling warmth steal through her at just the memory of it. Looking again at him, at the impossibly bland face that seemed to hold just a touch of mischief, she added quickly, 'And I think I might be wise to retreat while I'm ahead.'

Tossing back the rest of her drink, she got to her feet. 'Goodnight, Foster, and thank you.' As she walked past his chair, she looked down at him for a moment, and there was a very great temptation to drop a kiss on that warm mouth. Denying herself the thought of doing anything so stupid, she waggled her fingers at him, and went up to her room. She was behaving totally out of character, she thought crossly. She'd never been the sort of person to exchange casual hugs and kisses with people. Never. So why, in the name of all that was wonderful, did she want to start now? She was probably cracking up. Smiling to herself, she got ready for bed.

Another week slid past. Spring tried to make a stand, and was defeated by heavy storms that howled round the house day and night. Standing at her bedroom window, Zoe stared out into the garden. The trees were being whipped into a frenzy, thrashing madly about; rain hurtled suicidally against the window, then ran hastily down the pane as though it were late, late.

Heaving a big sigh, she traced her finger idly down the glass, and her mind conjured up the storm that had raged the night before her world ended. Then she gave a weak snort of amusement at the melodramatic phrase, but, for the first time since it had happened, she consciously summoned up the memory. If there hadn't been a storm then, the roads wouldn't have been littered with branches and wet leaves—and the tanker wouldn't have skidded. She'd stood frozen, her hand still in the post-box slot, the letter still in her fingers. She'd watched in disbelief and a numb kind of horror, knowing what was about to happen.

In slow motion, extraneous sounds blotted out, she had watched the tanker hurtle into the front of her shop, had watched it explode, and still she had stood, rooted to the spot as her livelihood, her home, had become a raging inferno. Had been only vaguely aware of people, of screams, shouts, police, ambulance, firemen, until Meg had led her away. And yet, now, it seemed almost as though it had happened to someone else. She ought to go back, see it, put it behind her. She also ought to go and see Meg. She'd been living in limbo long enough, and it was time to stop. Swinging away from the window, she ran downstairs.

She pushed open the study door and poked her head inside, then smiled faintly at the sight of Foster scowling horribly at the computer screen. He was muttering to himself, and she slipped inside and closed the door quietly behind her. Standing behind him, she peered over his shoulder.

'Problems?' she asked softly.

'Mm? Oh, no, not really, or not as long as I can figure out what that damned silly error message is, plastered across the screen.'

'It probably isn't anything,' she murmured. 'Sometimes, just like people, computers sulk or have temper tantrums. Press cancel.'

'I tried that, Miss Clever Clogs, it just beeped at me.'

'So beep back,' she recommended. 'I just came in to tell you that I was going out. I don't know what time I'll be back.'

'OK. Where are you going? Anywhere nice?' he asked absently, as he pressed various keys, all with the same result, more beeps.

'No, only going to see Meg. I should have gone before.'

'Yes, you should... Oh, hell, now what's it playing at?' With an abrupt movement that she might have called temper in anyone else, he removed the disc and shut the machine off.

'Well, there, that'll jolly well teach it to misbehave,' she said approvingly, then leapt backwards, laughing, as Foster swivelled round to face her, hands held out as though to grab her.

Subsiding back in his chair, he stared at her for long moments, his eyes amused. 'Want some company?' he suddenly asked.

'To go and see Meg?'

'Or the remains of the shop,' he murmured. 'That is what this is all about, isn't it?'

'Yes. But I'm all right and, to be honest, I think I'd rather go alone, come to terms with it once and for all. I don't know what time I'll be back, but I won't be late.'

'All right, Zoe. Take care, hm?'

''I will,' she promised, 'and thanks for not insisting, for allowing me to make my own judgements.'

'Why not? You're a big girl now.'

'Yes, I am. Unfortunately a lot of people fail to recognise that fact.'

'Men, you mean,' he taunted softly. 'Never make the mistake of judging me by others, Zoe Mitchell.' Which was something she most definitely wasn't in danger of doing, she thought in amusement. 'Go on, go away and leave me in peace.'

She arrived in the village around eleven, went to look at where her shop had once stood, and, to her surprise, didn't feel as upset as she'd expected. It was past and gone, and nothing would bring it back. In fact, Meg had seemed more concerned than Zoe herself, and discussed it constantly over lunch, bewailing and bemoaning the fact that Zoe was now homeless. Yet she didn't feel homeless; she seemed to have adapted to her life with Foster with no trouble at all, and certainly she no longer felt sad and lost, and had to fiercely squash her irritation with Meg for harping on the fact. With nothing further to keep her in Buckinghamshire, she drove thankfully back to Sussex—and to Foster, yet never once stopped to analyse fully why she felt so at home living with him.

In a new mood of resolution, the first thing she did when she got back was ring the insurance company. Meg had said the insurance assessors had been round a week previously, so it was about time that she heard something. For all they knew, she could be living in a tent! The more she thought about it, the more militant she felt. In fact, she told herself, they weren't being cautious, as they'd told her when she'd rung last week; they were being evasive! Well, no more: enough was enough. Hanging her jacket up, she went into the lounge and picked up the phone. Never mind Foster telling her he'd deal with it, she was quite capable of fighting her own battles. Which was exactly what it turned out to be, the argument becoming so heated that it brought Foster out of the study, and he leaned in the doorway watching her, a small smile on his handsome face. Slamming down the receiver in temper, she turned to glare at him.

'What?' he queried mildly.

'Don't ask!' she snapped, getting to her feet to walk agitatedly back and forth across the room. 'Not liable,' she muttered, 'I'll give them not bloody liable!' Coming to an abrupt halt, she glared at Foster again, as though it were all his fault. 'I'm going up to town, that's what I'm going to do! I'll...'

'Calm down...'

'I don't want to calm down!' she shouted, her blue eyes hard. 'I want to go and kick somebody! My God, you pay all those insurance premiums, this cover, that cover, and then they say, oh, so sorry, we do realise how inconvenient it is. Inconvenient?' she exploded. 'I'll give them inconvenient! They won't know which side is up by the time I've finished with them! Not liable! Do you know what they said? Do you?' she demanded. Not waiting for him to comment, she marched across to him and poked him in the chest. 'Not liable, they said. It's down to the tanker company! Huh!'

'Zoe,' he began, putting his hands on her shoulders.

'Don't,' muttered Zoe crossly, trying to twitch away.

'Be still,' he commanded, his hands hardening for a moment. 'Getting angry is fine, if it's controlled...'

'Oh, terrific, is that what you do? Channel your anger? Well, bully for you, I don't have the necessary patience...'

'So I'm beginning to discover,' he said coolly.

'Well, you surely didn't expect me to remain as I was at seven, did you—I grew up, Foster, and when you grow up you change. And I do have a temper! Boy, do I have a temper. If you expected a meek, biddable house guest, you're in for a shock! Want me to leave?'

'No, I do not want you to leave. Neither do I want you going off at half-cock, exhausting yourself and putting their backs up. I'll put it in the hands of my lawyers, let them sort it out. You just leave it be.'

'Oh, that's easy for you to say,' she muttered peevishly. 'You're not homeless. You don't have hardly a rag to your back. You ... And will you stop being so damned reasonable? I hate reasonable people! And don't smile at me like that! It's very irritating!'

'Then stop being ridiculous ...'

'I'm not being ridiculous! I give them a fortune in premiums, and then they turn round and say they're not liable, and you tell me to stop being ridiculous? Don't you think I'm entitled to be angry? You'd just calmly shrug, I suppose? You'd just say, "Oh, well, never mind, I'll soon make another million. Hey ho, another day, another dollar. Who needs insurance companies?" Well, I need insurance companies!' she yelled. 'I need a roof over my head. I need clothes, furniture. I need to be independent! I can't stay here forever ... And, if you're just about to tell me I can, don't!'

'I wasn't going to,' he said quietly.

'Good. Because you know how stupid that would be ...'

'Have you finished?' he asked mildly, one eyebrow raised.

'Yes. No. I don't know—I'm fed up.'

'So I gathered,' he said drily. 'Take the Major for a walk.'

'Foster! I don't want to take the Major for a walk!'

'Yes, you do,' murmured Foster with that infuriating half-smile of his.

'I don't!' she gritted. Shrugging away from him, she continued her angry perambulation around the room. 'You don't even seem surprised,' she muttered, coming to a halt before him.

'No. There was a similar case some years back...'

'So you had some idea this would happen? Well, thanks, you might have warned me. Is that why you asked me to stay?'

'No. Go and get your coat. Go on,' he added putting a finger across her mouth as she opened it to argue. 'Leave it to me, I'll get it sorted out.'

'I don't want to leave it to you,' she mumbled grumpily. 'I keep leaving it to you.'

'It's what I'm for.'

'Now you're being ridiculous...' Catching in time the warning glint in his eye, Zoe let her breath out in a humph. Twitching away, she walked into the hall to get her coat and the dog lead. She called the Major, slammed out of the back door and began walking towards the woods. Her temper carried her as far as the town, and she gave a rueful smile. Being angry sure did get you exercised. She couldn't remember the last time she'd walked so far, if ever. But at least she was beginning to think more positively.

Wandering down the High Street, the Major trotting obediently at her heels, she received some curious glances, and she supposed that word had gone round that David Campbell had a young woman staying with him. There were two shops empty, and she wondered what the rent would be. Pretty high, she imagined. Sussex was not a cheap place to live. Well, it wouldn't hurt to make enquiries. Walking along to the estate agents', she went inside. They were friendly and helpful—and curious about her relationship with Foster. Not that that surprised her. He was obviously very well known, even in a town some distance from his home.

Giving evasive answers to their questions, she went despondently out to the High Street. Well, that solved that problem. No way could she afford those prices. Maybe she could give tuition on people's own computers. But not in the country. She would need to be in a large town for that. Chewing her lip thoughtfully, she slowly made her way back to the house. Very slowly; the five miles felt as though they'd become ten.

Leaving the thirsty dog with Laura in the kitchen, she took off her coat and poked her head into the study.

'Hi,' she murmured tentatively.

Swinging round in his swivel chair, he surveyed her tousled form for a moment, his mouth quirked up at one corner. 'Hi. Feeling better?'

'I suppose.' Then, with a rueful smile, she plumped down in the other chair and thankfully kicked her shoes off her aching feet. 'I walked to the town, enquired about some vacant shops.'

'Too expensive?'

'Mm. I don't think I've ever walked so far in my life. How far did you say it was? Five miles?'

'Three, if you cut through the woods,' murmured Foster, tongue in cheek.

'I'd prefer it to have been five,' she reproved wryly. 'Sounds more impressive... I'm sorry if I was rude.'

'Apology accepted,' he said mildly.

Tilting her head on one side, Zoe regarded him solemnly for a moment. 'Are you always this blasted reasonable?' she asked on a spurt of laughter. 'I don't think I've ever met anyone so—so *amiable*. And yet why do I keep getting the feeling that you're playing a part?' she asked thoughtfully.

'I don't know. Why do you?'

'See? There you go again!' she said in exasperation. 'You're impossible.'

'I'm a lot of things,' he murmured smoothly.

'So I'm beginning to discover. Someone in the village asked me if I was quite wise to stay here. Among your other things, are you also some sort of Bluebeard?'

'What do you think?'

'I think,' she murmured slowly, 'that you would be whatever you damned well wanted to be. And I think there's not one person who would try to stop you.'

'Would you try to stop me?' he asked softly.
'If I became a sort of Bluebeard, I mean.'

'To me?' she squeaked in astonishment.

'Mm.'

Frantically suppressing the warmth his words
brought to her insides, she forced herself to
remain calm. With a supreme effort of will, she
tilted her head the other way while she pre-
tended to consider his words, then, with a
teasing smile that she hoped didn't look as false
as it felt, murmured, 'I'd probably lie back and
enjoy it.'

'Why?'

'Why? Because you're one hell of a sexy
man—and you look wickedly experienced,' she
answered, with a flippancy that she was very
far from feeling.

'Wickedly?' he queried, one eyebrow raised.

'Mm. Wickedly. Whether you would enjoy
it is, of course, another matter.'

'Yes. Am I likely to get the opportunity to
find out?'

'Do you want the opportunity?' she asked
in a husky little voice.

'Oh, yes,' he said softly, and her heart missed
a beat. Two beats, and the warmth that she
had just managed to suppress began to steal
across her insides. Was he joking? The fact that
he might fancy her had never occurred to her—
and now that it had been mentioned, she didn't
honestly know how she felt about it. Yes, she
did, she decided; she wanted to lie back and
enjoy it, and that would be a damned silly thing

to do, living as they both were under the same roof. Those sort of complications she could do without, unfortunately. Her eyes wide and fixed on his, she blinked to break the lethargy that was stealing over her.

'I think this conversation is getting dangerous,' she mumbled evasively. 'Laura asked what you'd like for dinner,' she added in a belated attempt to turn the subject.

'Chicken.'

With a weak gurgle of laughter, Zoe got to her feet. 'Sorry, she only has lamb or pork.' She heard the grunt of amusement he gave as she hastily escaped. But she was very thoughtful and not a little alarmed at the notion of Foster actually fancying her. If he had been telling the truth, of course, which wasn't necessarily the case.

CHAPTER THREE

'IF YOU want something to keep you occupied while you're deciding what to do, you could see what sort of a fist you can make of the nursery,' Foster murmured, as they sat at the table eating their meal. Roast lamb. Not chicken.

'But I don't know anything about plants,' exclaimed Zoe, astonished.

'Then learn,' he said arrogantly. 'There are some books in my study that I bought when I was going to deal with it. I just never got around to reading them.'

'You make it sound like an order,' she muttered, not sure that she particularly wanted to play with pots and bags of earth, although in truth the topic was a hell of a lot safer than the one they'd had in his study.

'It was merely a suggestion,' he said mildly. 'Don't be so defensive.'

With a small shrug, she gave him a rueful smile. 'All right,' she agreed dubiously. 'I suppose I could try. And it would be a way of paying you back—only don't blame me if I make a hash of it.'

'You won't,' he said, with such confidence that she stared at him in amazement.

'How do you know? I might be the world's worst when it comes to horticulture. Apart from which, those greenhouses are in a hell of a state—I'd need all sorts of equipment. New glass, bedding trays, loam, peat, heater unit...'

'Then get them,' he said, with slight impatience. Obviously not a man who needed, or wanted, things spelt out to him. When he made a decision, it was final. Win or lose, he didn't want to know the details. However, it wasn't her money which she would be spending, and she felt a decided reluctance to put him to any more expense on her behalf, especially as at the moment it seemed merely a whim.

'It will be expensive...'

'Zoe! I said get what you need! End of subject.'

Giving a little sigh of impatience, she returned her attention to the meal. End of subject, indeed. And she'd very much like to know how or why he got the impression that she was capable of running a nursery. Certainly it wasn't from anything she'd ever said.

The rest of the meal was eaten in silence, but she was aware of the glances he gave her from time to time—only she refused to respond. She was beginning to wonder if she hadn't made a serious mistake in coming to stay here. Certainly her childhood friend wasn't quite as she remembered him.

The next few days were taken up with having one of the greenhouses repaired, making trips

to local garden centres to crib ideas, asking the
advice of experts on which seeds to use and
what to grow—and, to her surprise, Zoe found
that she quite enjoyed herself. Her days were
taken up with the mechanics of it, her evenings
reading the gardening books. Certainly it kept
her busy, and she barely saw Foster until after
the first seeds were planted.

Then she found she didn't quite know what
to do until the seedlings grew big enough to be
planted out in the bedding trays. Presumably
start again with another lot so that she would
have a constant supply of plants, although she
found herself reluctant to do so until she had
seen how the first ones turned out. She supposed she ought to go round the local shops to
see if she could find a market for them, only
she wasn't as confident as Foster about her
ability actually to grow anything worth selling.
Running a nursery was a far cry from programming computers. Not so long ago, she
would have grasped the challenge and made it
work. The fire seemed to have destroyed not
only her home, but her confidence in herself
as well. Or maybe not her confidence, she admitted honestly, more like her staying power.

Despite the fact that she barely saw Foster,
when he went away for a couple of weeks—she
did not know where, because he did not tell
her—she found that she missed him. Rather
more than she would have expected. Laura had
offered to sleep in the house if she was nervous,

an offer she declined. She wasn't nervous, just missing the fact of Foster being there.

When he returned, she was surprised by the feeling of pleasure she experienced on seeing his tall figure climb from a taxi. Walking out of the greenhouse to intercept him as he strode towards the house, she smiled faintly. Was she already coming to depend on his presence for her well-being? If so, that could be very foolish.

'Hi,' she said warmly as she reached him. 'Have a good trip?'

'So-so,' he murmured with his half-smile, which widened rather sardonically as she took his case from his hand and accompanied him indoors. 'Wifely behaviour, Zoe? Not like you.'

'No,' she murmured with a self-deprecating grin, 'and I hate to have to admit it, but I missed you.'

'Or only missed the feeling of company?' he murmured back.

Smiling, refusing to answer, she asked instead, 'Want a cup of tea?' then thumped him on the arm when he grunted with laughter.

'Where's Laura?'

'She went home. One of her wretched cats was ill, and I'm quite capable of getting myself lunch. Or getting us lunch,' she amended.

'Mm. I didn't let you know because I didn't know myself until a short while ago that I'd be back today,' he stated drily.

'I wasn't reproving you,' she laughed. 'But it is nice to see you. Come and see what I've been up to.'

With her hand tucked companionably into his arm, she led him out to the greenhouse and proudly showed him the green shoots just beginning to peep through the soil. 'See? Success.'

'Mm. What are they?'

'Runner beans. When they get big enough and, hopefully, strong enough, I'll try and sell some to the garden shop in Petworth. Any that I don't sell I thought I might string along at the end of the greenhouse; then we can have fresh vegetables.'

'Wonderful,' he murmured. 'Just what I've always yearned for. Come and talk to me while I shower and change,' he added with a slight smile, and Zoe felt that odd feeling again in the pit of her stomach, the feeling which she had managed to squash all the time he'd been away.

Accompanying him back to the house, she tried to identify her chief emotion. A sort of fearful excitement, she decided. Glancing at him from the corner of her eye, she found that he had a small, amused smile on his mouth, and she wondered if he knew how he affected her. Or was beginning to affect her. He was a damned attractive man, and presumably not celibate. Had many women shared his bed? Taking a deep breath to try and stop the way her thoughts were moving, she followed him up to his room. She hadn't been in there before, and she stared round curiously. There were one or two nice pictures on the cream walls, oatmeal-coloured curtains and carpet, a darker

brown duvet on the king-sized bed, and she
hastily averted her eyes from its magnificent
proportions. She was by no means an inno-
cent, but she got the feeling that with this man,
she would always be one step behind.

'Stop looking so worried,' advised Foster
slowly, as he removed his tie. 'Talk is what I
said. And talk is what I meant. Unless you want
different?' he added softly, his dark eyes intent
on hers. 'Do you?'

'No,' she murmured quickly. 'Talking is
much safer.'

'Yes. It is.'

As he removed his jacket and kicked off his
shoes, she walked across to stare from the
window. 'Do you have a current—er—lady
friend?' she asked quietly.

'No.'

'Just that? No?' she asked, surprised,
swinging round to face him.

'Just that,' he murmured, 'and, if you were
expecting chapter and verse, you're going to be
very disappointed, Zoe. I don't tell tales.'

'You don't tell anything. I know no more
about you now than when I came.'

'No,' he said, as he slowly unbuttoned his
shirt and removed it. He looked amused, and
she scowled at him. Of their own volition her
eyes moved over his strong muscled chest. He
was tanned and the flesh looked warm and
smooth, and she swallowed a sudden dryness
in her throat.

'No,' he said softly, and her eyes flicked hastily back to his.

'No? No what?' She managed only the slightest tremor in her voice.

'No, don't play with fire,' he said very, very quietly. 'You're liable to get your fingers burnt.'

'I have no intention of playing with fire,' she said more strongly, her eyes determinedly holding his.

'Don't you?'

'No.'

'Pity,' he murmured. With the almost-smile, that seemed to hold a great many meanings, he turned and walked into the bathroom, and she heard the sudden rush of water as he turned on the shower. 'Talk to me about the nursery,' he ordered over the noise of the shower. 'Like it or hate it?'

Wandering over to the bathroom door so that she wouldn't have to shout, she said, 'Neither one nor the other,' while her mind busily speculated on what he had meant. She just wished he wouldn't keep making enigmatic statements. She liked to know exactly where she was, what people meant. Foster Campbell could be very irritating. 'What did you mean by pity?' she asked, deciding that if she didn't get the damned statement clarified she'd spend half the night worrying about it.

'What did you think I meant?' he asked, sounding for all the world as though he were laughing.

'If I thought I knew what it meant,' she retorted, exasperated, 'I wouldn't have damned well asked you!'

'I meant,' he said softly, as the shower was turned off and he emerged wearing a brown towel round his hips, 'that I might enjoy bandaging your fingers.'

'Foster! I do wish you wouldn't persist in talking in riddles. You were the one who told me not to play with fire!'

'So I was. Want to dry my back?' he asked outrageously.

'No! Dry your own back!'

'Quite sure?' he asked, with that damned Cheshire Cat smile again. 'You might find you liked it.'

'I also might find myself getting burnt!' she snapped.

'Ah.'

'God, Foster, you really are infuriating at times.'

'I know.' Reaching back into the bathroom for a small hand towel, he proceeded to rub his hair so that his voice came out muffled. 'What else do you find me, Zoe?'

'What?' she asked weakly.

His ruffled head emerging from the towel, which he then looped round his neck, he stared at her for a long moment. 'I asked what else you found me?'

'I know you did. I meant that I didn't understand the question,' she said quietly, that awful feeling of weakness invading her again.

'You once said that you weren't a romantic. True?'

'Yes.'

'That you found men, on the whole, exasperating, lacking in understanding...'

'I know what I said, Foster, but what I want to know is where this very odd conversation is supposed to be leading.'

'To a proposal,' he said bluntly, his voice still soft, his eyes still on hers, with no expression at all in the dark brown depths.

'A proposal of what?' she asked, bewildered.

'Marriage.'

'Marriage?' she whispered weakly, sinking down on to the edge of the bed. 'You're asking me to marry you?'

'Yes.'

'But why?' she asked, her mind now totally confused. 'You aren't in love with me. You're self-contained, self-sufficient, a complete person. You like your life the way it is. Why on earth do you want a wife?'

'Would you believe I was lonely?' he asked softly.

'No.'

'That I've grown accustomed to your face?'

'Have you?' she asked drily, amusement overshadowing her perplexity.

'Yes, I do believe I have,' he declared, his eyes suddenly full of humour. 'I'm thirty-four. I've done all the things I set out to do. I have more than enough money for my needs—and I have an urge to become respectable. Conform.

And a wife would be very useful,' he added, tongue in cheek.

'The only bit I believe about that piece of nonsense is the last part. Why would a wife be useful?' she asked bluntly. 'For beating? Swapping?'

'Oh, no, Tiger. I would never swap someone that belonged to me. Nor would I beat her.'

'Belonged?' she asked softly. 'Belong. Verb meaning possess. Is that what your wife would be? A possession?'

'In a way. To be cherished, protected, looked after, but also as a person in her own right with the independence to do as she pleased—within reason,' he qualified. 'By your own admission you aren't a romantic. You find most men inferior...'

'I didn't say inferior,' protested Zoe.

'...or needing to dominate,' he continued smoothly. 'I would be neither. I like you. You don't bore me—and you would be a considerable asset to me in business.'

'How?'

'I sometimes need to entertain. At the moment I take guests to restaurants, hotels. It isn't a very satisfactory arrangement. If I had a wife to organise everything, I could entertain here. Not only that,' he continued, leaning one broad shoulder against the bathroom door-frame, 'but people will say all sorts of things to a wife that they wouldn't say to a mistress—or a friend.'

'It sounds to me as though what you need is a spy. Is that it?'

'No. A delightful companion whose first loyalty is to me.'

'A business arrangement?' she asked carefully.

'Not necessarily,' said Foster slowly, his eyes holding hers. 'It would be no hardship to make love to you, Zoe.'

'Wouldn't it, indeed? And might I remind you that it takes two to tango?' she put in hastily, annoyed with herself for sounding so breathless.

'Yes. So it does,' he murmured, with that infuriating half-smile of his.

'And I might not want to, might I?'

'No-o, I suppose that is conceivable . . .'

'Foster! I think you must be the most arrogant man I've ever come across! Do you really think that, just because you decide it wouldn't be totally anathema to you to make love to me, I'll go all soft and gooey and fall at your feet?' At the gleam of unholy amusement in his eyes, she added loftily, 'Anyway, I personally have always found it vastly over-rated.'

'Always?'

'Yes.'

'But then you haven't made love to me—have you?'

'No, I haven't! Nor am I likely to, the way I feel right at this moment,' she snapped.

With a laugh that sounded genuine, he walked across to his briefcase and extracted a report. Tossing it on to the bed, he said, 'Glance through that for me, and tell me what you think, while I get dressed.'

Staring at him in disbelief, she said weakly, 'Foster, you can't just introduce subjects, then abandon them without...'

'Why can't I?' he asked softly, that hated gleam of amusement back in his eyes.

'Because you can't! That's why! It's, well, it's...'

'Irritating?' he asked helpfully.

'Yes, it is! Honestly, I could slap you sometimes.'

'Now?'

'No! Not now!' she exclaimed, startled into a laugh. 'Go away!'

'Certainly.' Collecting clean things from his wardrobe, he went back into the bathroom and closed the door, only to open it a second later to murmur, 'Read the report.' With a little chuckle, he closed the door again. This time it remained closed.

'Wretch,' she muttered, then with a sigh of exasperation, her mind whirling with his ridiculous proposal, she leaned over and picked up the report. Married indeed! Yet there was an odd warmth inside her, a little feeling of excitement. Only how could she believe that he was serious? The whole idea was ludicrous. He was ludicrous. Impossible man. Focusing her attention on the report, she opened it. She read the first page without taking in a word of it, then had to read it again. It concerned a computer company and, her attention caught, she pushed Foster and his odd behaviour from her mind. She was so absorbed in the report that she didn't even hear him come out of the bathroom. When she'd read the last page, she closed it and looked up, her face thoughtful.

'Well?' he asked.

'Tell me first why you need to know,' she insisted. 'Is it on the market?'

'Mm. I was approached when I was in Japan.'

'Is that where you've been? Japan?' she asked, surprised. Although why she should have been surprised she wasn't quite sure.

'Mm. So? Worth pursuing, do you think?'

'No,' she said confidently. 'Even if the asking price is low, which it should be, judging by the losses they made last year, their computers are rubbish. Cheap certainly, and would have a place in the market, but they're unreliable, and once word gets around people won't touch them.'

'Mm. OK, come on, I could murder a pint,' and, taking the report out of her hands, he tossed it back on the bed.

'You'd take my word for it?' she asked slowly, staring from the report to him and back again.

'Of course—you know about computers, don't you?'

'Yes.'

'Well, then.' Extending a hand to her, he pulled her to her feet. 'We'll have something to eat out.'

'Will we?' she asked, still somewhat bemused as she brought her attention back to the present.

'Yes.'

Giving him a look of exasperation, she stared down at her jean-clad legs and the navy sweater that seemed to have specks of loam decorating the front, and smiled wryly.

'You might have said so earlier. I'll have to change, it won't take a minute.'

'You look fine as you are,' he said with a trace of impatience. 'We're only going to the pub. Just wash your hands or something.'

'Or something,' she murmured drily. 'Give me two minutes,' she instructed, firmly walking ahead of him out of the room, 'and I'll meet you downstairs.'

Going into her room, she quickly washed her hands, and wiped some cleanser over her face before changing into a navy and white striped sweater, then dragged the brush through her unruly hair. Unfortunately, the vigorous use of the brush only increased the static electricity, and the hair crackled and stood out from her head like a bush. Grimacing, she attempted to flatten it with her hands, then gave up. The two minutes had probably been and gone. Hurrying downstairs, still trying to flatten her hair, she gave Foster a wry grin as he leaned on the banister post at the bottom of the stairs, his chin on his hands.

'Now what's wrong?' he asked sardonically.

'Nothing, except that I look like Charles II. I've never understood why people always yearn for curly hair, it's a damned nuisance. I think I'll get it cut short.'

'And then you'll look like a Botticelli angel,' he murmured with a grin. 'Leave it alone, I like it like that—and it's not Charles II you look like, it's Marie Helvin.'

'Ooh, a compliment yet,' she quipped, to cover up the pleasure she felt at his words. Not that they were true, she looked nothing like Marie Helvin. Unfortunately.

Shaking his head at her, Foster whistled to the dog, then held his hand out to her. When, after a small hesitation, she curled her fingers in his, he tugged her out through the kitchen and began walking down the lane towards the pub. 'As my wife,' he continued, as though the subject had never been abandoned, 'you'd be able to do as you pleased, or almost. Pursue a career.'

'And what if that career needed to be pursued elsewhere?' she asked drily.

'Then we'd move. I can work anywhere.'

'I see. You've worked it all out, have you?'

'Yes, Zoe, I've worked it all out,' he confirmed, pushing open the door of the Grey Duck. 'What will you drink?'

'Gin and tonic,' she murmured faintly.

'Ploughman's? Sandwich? Packet of crisps?' he asked blandly.

'Ploughman's,' she said shortly. Feeling peeved, for no very good reason that she could discover, she sat at a vacant table by the wall. Why did he really want a wife? she wondered. There had to be more to it than he'd volunteered. Not that she had any intention of accepting his absurd proposal, although he most definitely ought to wear a sign on his back, she decided. This man is dangerous.

When he returned with their drinks, she tried to keep her face as blank as his usually was. She wasn't sure that she succeeded. Not wishing to plunge into another confusing conversation, she picked up her drink and stared round her. The pub wasn't full, by any means. A couple of workmen in jeans and donkey jackets with Murphy written on the back were propping up the bar. There was a young man who looked as though he might be a bank clerk, and three young girls at the next table, their heads close together, whispering. About the bank clerk? she wondered. Eyeing the local talent?

'What's amusing you?' Foster asked softly.

'Oh, just speculating on who the girls were whispering about. I thought it might be the bank-clerk type at the bar, but I see two young men across the far side who seem to be casting longing glances in their direction,' she murmured absently. 'How long do I have to consider your—er—proposal?' she asked.

'As long as you like,' he answered, sounding amused. 'I expected a flat no.'

'I rarely give flat nos,' she retorted with a faint smile. 'I like to consider my options. Although why I'm even considering this one heaven alone knows. It's the craziest thing I've ever heard. Are you really serious about this?'

'Oh, yes, Zoe. I'm serious.'

'And you feel quite well? It's not jet-lag? Fever? A dizzy spell?'

'No. Nary a one... It can be a purely business arrangement if the thought of being intimate with me troubles you,' he said very softly. 'Does it?'

Feeling a little ripple of shock run through her, because she hadn't actually considered that aspect of it, she dragged her eyes away from his, and stared blindly down into her drink. 'I don't know,' she whispered.

'But might be willing to find out?' he pressed, his voice still soft, seductive almost.

'I don't know that, either,' she confessed, 'although the problem doesn't really arise, does it? Because I can't honestly see myself marrying you,' she said staunchly. 'And you can take that damned smirk off your face, Foster! I think the whole stupid subject ought to be abandoned.'

'All right,' he said amiably, and she stared at him suspiciously, then glared at the barman when he brought their ploughman's lunches over, as though it were his fault that she was feeling so confused. While they ate, Foster discussed business, long-haul flights, even computers, anything and everything, it seemed, except the subject that was filling her mind. She supposed she answered sensibly, goodness knew how.

She spent the afternoon in the greenhouse re-potting things that didn't need re-potting. Cleaning tools that were already sparkling. Unfortunately, it didn't stop her whirling thoughts. How did she feel about allowing him to make love to her? she wondered, probing her thoughts like a wobbly tooth. Even the thought of it made her feel weak, and she sank down on to the little stool. Yet why should it trouble her? As she'd told him, she considered making love a vastly overrated occupation. Or it had been with Peter. But would it be that way with Foster? She got the feeling that it most definitely wouldn't. Conjuring up an image of his mouth, she tried to imagine it touching hers in passion. In a determined assault on her senses—and she shuddered. She could still very clearly remember how she had felt when she'd only briefly touched her mouth to his.

Yet even apart from that, even if they didn't have an intimate relationship, could she live with him? As she was beginning to discover, he only let her see that part of his personality that he wanted her to see. And that, she knew, was only the tip of the iceberg. Did he have a temper? She suspected that he did. Not a shouting, violent sort of temper, but a cold, calculating, hurting anger that would destroy the recipient. He was ruthless, arrogant, contained. He was also generous, kind in an offbeat way. Thoughtful. But marriage? To a man like Foster? To sleep with him? Make love with him? Covering her hot cheeks with her hands, she stared blindly at the bench. To have that strong, tough body curled warmly against hers? Oh, hell.

When she went back to the house, she avoided looking at him, afraid almost that he might guess the way her thoughts had been running. But when he made no comment, behaved as he normally behaved, she gradually relaxed. Yet, as the days slipped past without him mentioning it further, she found herself becoming thoroughly irritated and on edge. Perhaps he'd only been teasing her? Yet she found that she didn't quite like that explanation, and she took to watching him until his bland smiles drove her insane. He'd lodged the damned idea in her mind, and now she couldn't get it out again. He was either a fool, which she couldn't believe, or a master tactician, which she could.

A whole week passed without his broaching the subject that had kept her awake at nights, until she almost reached the point of mentioning it herself; and then, of course, the very moment she'd persuaded herself to forget it, to put it out of her mind for good, Foster brought up the subject himself, when she was least expecting it.

CHAPTER FOUR

THE evenings were still chilly and they were sitting before the fire, Foster on the sofa, Zoe on the floor at his feet. She was leafing through a seed catalogue, wondering if by any stretch of the imagination her plants would ever look like those depicted. Foster was reading the annual report and accounts of one of the companies of which he was a shareholder. Feeling a light touch on her hair, she looked up in query, and the expression on his face locked the breath in her throat.

'Foster?' she questioned uncertainly.

Without answering, he took the brochure out of her hand, and dropped it on the floor. 'Come here,' he ordered softly.

With her heart fluttering unevenly, she twisted round and came to her knees.

'All the way.'

Swallowing drily, she levered herself on to the sofa beside him. 'What?'

'This,' he said softly. Sliding a warm palm beneath her thick dark hair, he bent his head and touched his mouth infinitely gently against hers, making her shiver. His other arm slid round her waist and drew her closer, so that her head was resting against his shoulder. His mouth touched hers again and again, softly, teasingly, and she closed her eyes. As his mouth claimed hers more insistently, she slowly released her pent-up breath and relaxed into his hold. It was a practised lesson in seduction, but none the less exciting for that. She tried to remain as objective as she guessed he was, and failed. His kisses were warm and soft, comforting and moreish, she decided hazily. When he broke the kiss, she mumbled a complaint. Opening her eyes, she saw that he was smiling faintly.

'Nice?' he asked softly.

'Mm.'

'But clinical?'

'Not on my side,' she murmured huskily. 'I feel as soft and supple as a cat. Whatever you turn your hand to, you always make sure you're very good, don't you? Even if it's only kissing.'

'Only kissing? Is that reproof I hear in your voice, Tiger?'

Pushing her hand between them, she rubbed her thumb across his lower lip. 'I feel you could do better,' she taunted, probably not very sensibly, but she had a sudden desire to know what it would be like to be kissed properly by this enigmatic man.

'I was practising caution,' he explained, against her hand. 'However...'

'Why?'

'Why was I practising caution? Or why did I kiss you?' he asked, those dark, usually unfathomable brown eyes full of humour.

'The latter.'

'To see if we were compatible, of course,' he murmured lazily. 'I thought your reluctance to consider my proposal might be because you weren't sure how you would react to my touch.'

'Oh, did you?' asked Zoe softly, knowing that he was referring to the little episode in the hall when she had run away like a startled rabbit. 'But might not my hesitation, as you call it, be because I value my independence?'

'It might. Is it?'

'I don't know,' she said, with a soft, lazy smile as she happily traced the line of his mouth with her forefinger. 'I agreed to marry Peter because I thought I was in love with him. I'm not in love with you—nor are you in love with me. I like you, enjoy your company...'

'Well, that's comforting,' he murmured, with his infuriating half-smile.

Giving him a look of exasperation, she continued, 'Supposing I did marry you, then some time in the future I met someone else. What then?'

'Then I would release you,' he said simply.

'Would you?' she asked, her voice reflecting her disbelief. 'Don't I seem to remember you talking about possessions?'

'I wouldn't hold you against your will, Zoe. That would be a fool's game. And I'm not a fool.'

'No. You're not a fool. So I begin to wonder why you want to tie yourself up to someone you barely know.'

'I've met and known some exceptionally beautiful women in my life. Some from ordinary backgrounds, some with a life-style I have no wish to emulate, or join. Night-clubbing and partying bore me . . . As do most women,' he added softly. 'My fault, I expect, but I have no time for vanity, pomposity, for the shallow existence that a lot of them pursue. Not all, certainly. Some beautiful women I've met have been intelligent, witty and delightful companions. Unfortunately, those are the ones that are already married. I've been involved with one or two women, but never emotionally. Again, my fault. My life has not always been easy, and perhaps my yardstick is longer or tougher than most people's. I want, need women sometimes, but I've never wanted a lasting attachment. Now you, Zoe,' he added with his half-smile, 'don't seem to fit into any of those categories. You are astonishingly beautiful—hair the colour of midnight,' he said, quietly pushing one hand into the tumbled mass, 'eyes of deepest sapphire . . . You're intelligent, amusing. You do not expect, or ask, for anything. You cope. You don't irritate me. Most people do. I doubt that I will change, become a romantic, fall in love. So, having met you again, remembered your spunk, your loyalty . . .'

'You arrogantly decided that I would make a splendid candidate,' she finished for him.

'Mm. You also have a mouth that is eminently kissable. Now list all your reasons, logical and illogical, for refusing.'

'I can't,' she said simply. 'My reasons are nebulous, they have no foundation. If I'm totally honest, my mind won't even settle to the problem—it shies away each time I try to consider it.'

When Foster didn't respond, but merely continued to regard her intently, she gave a soft sigh. 'I think I'm afraid I might have a tiger by the tail,' she confessed, 'and, although I can appreciate your reticence at the moment, I am after all only a guest in your house, and you owe me nothing. I don't think I could cope with it if I were your wife. You never explain, you make odd statements—and I think, eventually, it would drive me insane.'

'Mm.'

'See? There you go again. Mm, indeed. What's that supposed to mean?'

'Whatever.'

'Exactly! And you won't promise to change or clarify things for me, will you?'

'No.'

'No. It didn't seem to be a problem at seven. I made up my fantasies about you, and to me, they were real—only I grew up, Foster, and fantasies aren't so easy to believe in.'

'No. But then the reverse is also true. I shan't expect you to explain your actions or reasons to me. I shan't constantly demand to know where you're going, where you've been. Because if you're honest, my friend, you wouldn't like it any more than I do. Would you?'

'No,' she admitted wryly.

'So you see, it wouldn't be any different from now—except that you would be my wife.'

'Yes. Except that I would be your wife,' she echoed softly.

'Yes.'

'Why do I keep getting the feeling that I'm missing something?'

'I don't know. May we now get back to being compatible?' he asked, that flicker of humour again moving in his eyes.

'I get a choice?'

'Oh, yes, Zoe, there's always a choice.'

Moving her eyes to his mouth, she stared at the slightly full lower lip, at the determined chin below it, then back to his eyes. Would those blank eyes soften in passion? Would the harsh planes of his face relax? Would he ever murmur endearments? Words of love? Did she even want that? Here was a man that many women would kill for. Wealthy, devastatingly attractive and as deep as the deepest part of the ocean, and she doubted that anyone would ever know him completely. They might think they knew him, understood him, but they never would. She doubted that he even understood himself. This was the boy whom she had defended, championed. This was the boy in the cheap clothes, with the still face, the everwatchful eyes. This was her friend, still was her friend—and she suddenly smiled at him. A warm, uncomplicated smile. 'Then kiss me, Foster, do your damnedest to convince me we're compatible.'

'And then you'll marry me?'

'No,' she grinned. 'Then I'll think about it... Besides,' she added, with a teasing glint in her lovely eyes, 'it's a long time since I've been kissed so nicely, and I never was one to let a good opportunity go to waste. So kiss me,' she breathed enticingly, on a little gurgle of laughter.

'Pleasure.'

And it was. For her, anyway, though she was never quite sure about him. He parted her mouth by exerting gentle pressure on her chin with his thumb, then touched his mouth lightly against hers, touched again, teasing her, tantalising. With a little sigh of enjoyment, she relaxed against him, winding her arms round his strong back. The kiss deepened with a barely perceptible pressure, his tongue traced the outer edge of her mouth—and then he lifted his head, leaving her dazed, disorientated, and with a marked reluctance to open her eyes, until he blew softly on the lids.

'More,' she mumbled thickly.

'Sure.'

Holding her head between his large palms, he kissed her, thoroughly, expertly, excitingly, and she burrowed closer to his warm body, tightening her arms around him until nothing existed except the warmth of his lips on hers, the feel of his tongue in her mouth, the gentle touch of his fingers at her nape, the steady rise and fall of his chest against hers. The rise and fall of her chest wasn't steady, but decidedly erratic, her breathing laboured.

'Compatible,' he murmured. A statement, not a question.

'So it would seem,' she breathed huskily, staring into deep brown eyes that stared blandly back, 'and it didn't affect you at all, did it?'

'Oh, yes, Zoe,' he said softly, 'it affected me.'

Moving her hand from his back, she rested it over his heart. The beat was even and strong, not accelerated at all. 'Fibber.'

'No... Just iron control,' he responded, with a small amused smile.

'I don't think I believe you.'

'Do I care?' he asked softly.

'No, I don't suppose you do.'

'Want to practise some more?'

'Isn't that rather dangerous?'

'For whom?'

Staring up at him, she swallowed drily. 'For me. I don't know where it might lead.'

'It won't lead anywhere you don't want it to,' he reassured her quietly. Sliding his arms loosely round her, he drew her gently against him, his eyes staring down into her own. 'Put your hands on my shoulders—kiss me—gently, softly, tormentingly. No hassle, no haste, just your mouth touching mine.'

'That sounds positively erotic,' she mumbled shakily.

'Mm. Love it.'

With a grunt of laughter, she scrambled to her knees, then pushed him backwards. Lying across him as he lay full length on the sofa, she slid her hands into his thick dark hair, luxuriated in the feel of it between her fingers, and, although she wasn't nearly so experienced as he obviously was, she felt that she didn't do too badly, as far as kissing went. But she had no intention of allowing it to go any further, and as she felt her body change, begin to melt, as his arms tightened fractionally, she called a halt, rolled away and got to her feet. Her breathing ragged, she stared down at him, at the tousled hair, the still face, and she whispered softly, 'Goodnight, Foster.' Because if she stayed, just one moment more, it wouldn't end at kissing.

Turning swiftly, she walked out and upstairs to her room. Standing at her window, one hand to her mouth, she stared blindly into the night. She thought she had probably been a bit stupid. Her breathing was still erratic, her heart thudding heavily in her breast. If he could make her feel like this when he was being restrained, how would he make her feel when he wasn't? Peter had never made her feel like this. She felt positively wanton. With a small groan, she got ready for bed. It was a long time before she fell asleep.

'Marry me,' he said softly, as they met on the landing the next morning.

'No,' she said, equally softly.

With a small smile, he ran lightly down the stairs and into this study. 'Call me for breakfast,' he said over his shoulder, before closing the door. Her smile an echo of his, she walked down more slowly and pushed into the kitchen. No Laura. Odd; it was not like Laura to be late. Opening the back door to let the dog out, Zoe peered along the track that Laura always used to get from her house to Foster's, and then felt a distinct *frisson* of alarm as the Major roared off down the lane, barking furiously. It wasn't his usual exuberant barking when he was let out. This had a distinctly menacing sound to it.

Not bothering to put anything on her feet, she began to run. It didn't even occur to her to get Foster. When the dog's barking turned to growls, she slowed cautiously, and, as she turned the bend in the track, she halted. The Major's teeth were bared and his hackles up as he confronted two men—boys really, they looked to be in their early twenties—but one of them had a gun. It was pointed at the dog.

Her heart thumping unnaturally fast, she approached slowly, advancing until she was beside the Major. Staring at the young man with the gun, she said, softly and very clearly, 'Put that down,' and, when he turned to face her, a mixture of fear and arrogance on his face, she added in the same quiet tone, 'You harm one hair of that dog, and I personally will kill you.' She didn't think she had ever been so angry. Her eyes holding his, she deliberately took hold of the barrel, and pushed it to one side. And then she saw Laura. Without thought, without consideration, she pushed past both men and went to kneel by the housekeeper.

'I think I broke my leg,' Laura whispered. Her face was the colour of old parchment, a long scratch on her cheek where she had fallen against the bush where she still lay.

'Give me your coat,' she said to the man nearer her.

'What?'

'Give me your bloody coat!' she snapped. With a blank look at his companion, who had the gun, the man took off his coat and handed it across. 'Thank you.' Wrapping it warmly round Laura, Zoe turned back in exasperation. 'Well, don't just stand there, go up to the house and ring for an ambulance!'

'For all you know, we could be burglars, rapists...' the man with the gun began.

'I don't give a damn what you are—at this precise moment all I want is for one of you to go for an ambulance! Now, move! And put that stupid gun down before it goes off!'

With a shrug, he motioned the other man to go along to the house. 'Call the dog off, and I'll put the gun down,' he said quietly, and she looked at him speculatively.

'I do hope that's not a threat,' she said, equally quietly, and wondered fleetingly why she didn't feel afraid. Turning to the dog, she said authoritatively, 'Sit!' Much to her surprise, the Major did. His teeth were still bared, his hackles still up, and he still growled menacingly in the back of his throat, but he sat— and then Foster was there, followed by the man who had gone to the house. Foster didn't waste time asking stupid questions, demanding answers, but just looked coldly at the man with the gun, patted the Major's head, and then came to squat beside Zoe and Laura.

'The ambulance is on its way,' he said quietly and, making a fist, gently touched it to Laura's chin. 'Fall?'

'Yes. I came across them unexpectedly, lost my balance. They didn't touch me. If they had, I think Zoe would have killed them single-handed. Or the Major.' With a wan smile for Zoe, she put out a hand which Foster grasped warmly. 'I'm sorry.'

'So I should think,' answered Foster, with a small comforting smile.

'If they keep me in, what shall I do about the cats?' she asked, worried, even in pain, for her animals.

'What you will do is not worry. The cats will be looked after. I promise.'

'Thank you.'

Foster gave Laura's hand into Zoe's, and stood to confront the two intruders. 'If you were intending to shoot on my land, don't,' he said softly. 'Now go.'

'She's got my coat.' But the man didn't say it aggressively, or arrogantly, or with any demand that Foster should immediately return it. Nor would Zoe have done, if he were ever to look at her the way he was looking at the two men. She thought she might have died of fright.

'Then stand to one side until the ambulance arrives. Move slowly, quietly, without alarming the dog. And unload that gun.'

They did exactly as they were told, and within a few minutes the ambulance could be heard. 'Zoe, go and direct it, please.'

Zoe did.

'We'll be along to the hospital in a few minutes,' Foster reassured Laura. Giving her hand a warm squeeze as she was loaded into the ambulance, he returned the coat to one of the men. 'Don't come back, ever.' With a curt nod, he indicated that they should leave.

'You don't have any shoes on,' he said mildly, turning to Zoe.

'No,' she said lamely.

'You also behaved like a damn fool.'

'Yes.' And for a bit of British understatement that surely had to be a masterpiece. Damn fool, indeed, more like lunatic.

'Thank you.' With a smile that was warm and almost brilliant, Foster added, 'I'm exceedingly hungry... And I want to make love to you.'

With a soft laugh that was only the tiniest bit shaky, she leaned against him, and pressed her mouth into his warm neck. 'Oh, Foster, you can't.'

'Can't I? Oh, all right,' he murmured on a thread of laughter. Hugging her to his side, he led her and the dog back to the house.

Zoe washed her muddy feet, and pulled on socks and boots. She ran a brush through her hair, and then went quickly downstairs, where Foster was waiting to drive them to the hospital. After making enquiries in Casualty, they had some breakfast in a little nearby café, before returning to wait for news of the housekeeper. Fortunately, her ankle wasn't broken, just sprained, and they were allowed to take her home with them.

'I'll see if I can get someone to go in each day to see to Laura's needs,' he said, after they'd dropped her off at her cottage because she had categorically refused to stay at Foster's house.

'You already have someone.'

'So I do,' he said softly, turning to give her a smile that made her heart race.

Pulling a face at him, she murmured, 'I'll go down to her house each morning, let the cats in or out, whichever way round it is, feed them of an evening. It will only be for a few days. The doctor thought she'd be able to get around by the end of the week.' Zoe knew that she was babbling, but the look in Foster's eyes was very unnerving, and she had the oddest desire to press her mouth to his. Be held in his strong arms, let him make love to her—as he had professed a desire to do. 'And you'll never know,' she continued hastily, 'how noble a

gesture that is. I hate cats—and they know it.
I can guarantee that, if there's a room full of
moggy lovers, the cat will make a bee-line for
me. It never fails. Very perverse creatures are
cats.'

'Mm. Want me to do it?'

'Certainly not; I shall look on it as a challenge.' And if you don't stop looking at me like
that, there'll be another challenge thrown
down, she thought confusedly. It seemed to be
the hungry look of a large animal about to
devour its prey.

When she came back from feeding the cats that
evening, Foster was in the kitchen, of all places,
actually cooking a meal.

'Think I couldn't?' he asked, when she stared
at him in astonishment.

'I don't think I thought about it at all. And
I don't know why I'm surprised. I shouldn't
be.'

'No,' he murmured softly. 'Feed the cats all
right?'

Extending for his inspection one hand with
a long scratch decorating the back, she said
wryly, 'Remind me to keep my mouth shut in
future.'

'Attacked you *en masse* did they?'

'Close. One took exception to the amount of
time it took me to open the tin. He won't do
it again,' she said, in some satisfaction. 'That
is one moggy who has learnt his lesson.'

'What did you do? Slap his paw?'

'Not his paw, no.'

'Tut, tut, cruelty to animals.'

'What about cruelty to humans?' she asked in mock outrage. 'Anyway, it was only a gentle wallop, which under the circumstances I thought very restrained of me... What delicacy do we have for dinner? I'm starving.'

'Shepherd's pie. Go and lay the table.'

'Yes, sir.' Throwing up a mock salute, she went to do as she was told, a small smile on her mouth.

When she returned from Laura's the next morning, after seeing to the invalid's needs and collecting her shopping list, it was to find a strange woman standing in the hall. She was thin almost to the point of emaciation, with grey hair scragged back with no attempt at style, and a thin, pointy face that reminded Zoe of a picture she had once seen of a Victorian governess who lived and died by the scriptures. Giving her a lame smile, Zoe sidled into the study and quietly closed the door.

'Who's that?' she hissed.

'Mrs Bates,' Foster informed her with a droll look.

'Oh, that figures. Norman's mother lives on,' and at his faint look of puzzlement, explained, '*Psycho*. Norman Bates, Motel of Horror...'

'Oh.'

'You haven't the faintest idea what I'm talking about, have you?' she grinned. 'Didn't you ever see the film?'

'Er—no. I'm ashamed to confess that I never go to the cinema.'

'No,' she agreed with a grin. 'I can't quite see you cramped up in the three and nines. She is presumably replacing Laura?'

'Just temporarily,' he drawled. 'Good help is hard to find.'

'Well, if that's the best, heaven help those who have the worst.' Words she came to revise over the next few days. The worst of the worst couldn't have been more infuriating than Mrs Bates.

She also seemed to have taken a dislike to Zoe which took the form of persecution. Wherever Zoe was, a few minutes later there also was Mrs Bates, flicking her feather duster around as though her very life depended upon it.

Laura was naturally delighted, and gained a great deal of amusement from Zoe's scathing comments on the behaviour of her temporary replacement.

'I think she thinks I give off large quantities of dust! Even if I'm sitting perfectly still, she flicks and flitters round me like a demented bee! I'm being driven from the house! Foster thinks it's hysterical...' Then she gave a lame grin at Laura's disbelieving expression. 'Well, he would,' she qualified, 'if he allowed his face to crack far enough. I don't think I've ever met anyone who hides their thoughts so well.'

Then Zoe spent a good five minutes staring into space, while she wondered what the hell

she was going to do about Foster. She caught
him looking at her sometimes with a very odd,
brooding expression on his face. Perhaps he
was wondering what to do about her? Whatever
the reason, she was beginning to find the habit
rather unnerving, and in truth was quite glad
to get out of the house, Mrs Bates or no Mrs
Bates, because if she stayed in the house she
was going to end up doing something exceedingly stupid, like letting him make love to her.
Things were beginning to happen in the greenhouse, which was a good excuse to stay out of
his way, and so, with that and Laura to look
after, she managed to avoid him quite nicely
without making it too obvious that she was
doing so. But she had the horrible feeling that
she was the only one to suffer.

Staring round her little domain, she saw that
there were now quite a few shoots to transfer
to seedling trays. Larger plants to pot. New
seeds to be put in. So why wasn't she satisfied?
she wondered. Because it wasn't challenging
enough? Because it didn't stimulate her mind?
Not that she had any intention of admitting it
to Foster. Some ingratitude that would be, after
he'd been so kind. Although she might have
known that he wouldn't need telling, even if
he hadn't found her wrestling crossly with the
heater one evening.

'I did not intend, when I suggested this, that
you should spend each and every hour in here,'
he said quietly, from the doorway.

'I don't spend each and every hour in here, as you put it. I'm only out here now because the stupid heater keeps going off, and if I don't keep the plants at an even temperature, they'll die. And don't say it isn't important, because it is.'

'Then I'll get someone to run it...'

'You will not! I've worked damned hard in here, and I'm not about to turn over the fruits of my labour to someone else!' Zoe crossly snatched from his hands one of the trays which was unfortunately filled with wilting seedlings.

'Fruits?' he taunted softly, the hated smile playing about his mouth.

'So I've had a few minor mishaps,' she said loftily. 'Perfection takes a while to achieve.'

Shaking his head at her, he turned to leave, taunting over his shoulder, 'So does trying to avoid me,' and very nearly got the seed tray thrown at his head. 'Come and see me in the study when you've finished.'

'Dictator,' she muttered peevishly.

When she'd washed her hands, she walked slowly along to his study. Pushing open the door, she leaned her shoulder against the frame, and eyed him warily.

'Come and sit down,' he ordered softly.

When she'd done so, he astonished her all over again by saying, 'Meads, one of the companies I own, wants to install a new computer system. Want to check it out for me?'

Her mind scrabbled uselessly as she tried to grasp that the rules of the game had changed, and she blindly took the file he was holding out, then glanced down at it. With a determined effort, she read the first page. It was a system which she actually knew something about. 'I'd need to know more about the company's requirements before recommending it,' she commented.

'Then go and see them, talk to the finance man, the accounts, the managing director. Talk to the operators, to whomever you think necessary. Then come back to me with a recommendation.'

'You'd really trust me to do all this?' she asked, amazed.

'Of course.'

'All right,' she said slowly. Looking back at him, she gave a little nod. 'All right,' she said more positively. 'I think I'd enjoy that.'

'Mm. Thought you might. Certainly it will take your mind off other things, won't it?' he asked softly.

Poking her tongue out at him, she settled down to read the report. She'd need to understand their reasoning, their requirements, before going to see them. For the first time in weeks there was a purposeful air about her, and Foster gave a small smile of satisfaction.

CHAPTER FIVE

At Foster's insistence Zoe bought herself a smart navy suit, navy heeled shoes and matching leather bag. To act the part, you have to look the part, he'd murmured, and she was forced to agree. She'd also bought some make-up. She'd never bothered to replace her own after the fire because it seemed an unnecessary extravagance on Foster's money, but now she could justify it by wanting to look her best. Dark blue shadow and mascara skilfully applied, translucent powder, blusher and a deep pink lipstick that exactly matched the shirt which she had bought to wear under the suit. Having gone that far, she naturally had to buy nail varnish as well. Not that her poor nails did justice to it. Gardening had ruined them. When she was ready, she walked into the study for his inspection. Giving a little twirl, she waited expectantly.

'What do you want me to say, Tiger?' he asked softly.

'That I look nice?' she asked hopefully, a smile in her eyes.

'You presumably have just been preening in front of a mirror, so you know how you look,' he said, straight-faced. 'Don't you?'

Unable to hold her pout, she gave a gurgle of laughter. 'Yes. But a gentleman would have complimented me without prompting.'

'Go away,' he said softly. 'Have a nice day.'

Laughing, she went out to her car. Foster had promised to keep an eye on Laura and the cats, leaving her free to take her own time without the need to rush back home. He'd told her to head for Chichester, then pick up the major road for Portsmouth. With the directions he'd given her stuck on the dashboard in front of her, and feeling almost as though she were going on holiday, she drove confidently towards her destination.

She spent a thoroughly enjoyable day, poking, prying, talking to people, getting to know the layout of the place, and returned home late that evening. She refused to discuss it with Foster until she'd made a thorough assessment—not that he asked her to discuss it, she thought wryly, just mentioned that he'd seen Laura, fed the cats, and then wished her a cheerful goodnight, which left her feeling thoroughly dissatisfied and sort of empty.

When she left for Meads again the following morning, he merely told her to drive carefully. Not sure if she was peeved or flattered, she drove back to Portsmouth, and spent another enjoyable day, her confidence growing hour by hour. She went through the report with the finance director. Suggested changes, a slightly modified approach, cost-cutting without removing any effectiveness, because to be too economic, cut corners, wouldn't in the end create the efficiency they needed. When she was satisfied that they'd covered all the points, she asked that they type up a new report and submit it. She'd get Foster's approval, and get back to them.

When she returned to the house, a new lightness in her step, a more confident gleam in her eyes, she sought Foster out in his study. He was leaning back in his swivel chair, a small smile on his face, and she wanted to hug him. 'No, yes, no,' he murmured, his eyes amused.

'I beg your pardon?' she asked, startled, wondering for a moment if he'd read her thoughts.

'No, I do not wish to discuss it. Yes, I will accept your recommendations. No, I do not want the details.'

'Just like that?' she asked, laughing in relief and collapsing back into the other chair, crossing her long legs.

'Just like that,' he confirmed.

Giving him a long, contemplative look, her dark blue eyes amused, she murmured, 'Just when I think nothing you do will surprise me, you surprise me. Thank you.'

'Enjoy yourself?'

'Yes. Immensely.'

'Good. Welcome back to the world.'

Looking surprised for a moment, she suddenly smiled. 'Been that bad, have I?'

'No, just a little lost-looking.'

'Have I? I'm sorry. I never meant to be a misery.'

'You haven't,' he denied. 'Just a bit introspective, I think.'

'Mm,' she murmured evasively. If she had, it wasn't because of the fire, but because of his odd, distracting behaviour. Deliberately changing the subject, she asked, 'You don't want to eat for a while?'

'Why? Are you hungry?'

'No, I'd like to check over my notes first.'

'Heavy business lunch?' he teased softly, his eyes amused.

Giving him a sweet smile, she returned 'If you'll excuse me, I'll go and get started. I asked them to submit a new report.' Then she walked out, and into the sitting-room. Taking her papers from the briefcase that she'd borrowed from Foster, she settled herself on the sofa— and, not two minutes later, Mrs Bates appeared with the inevitable feather duster.

'Mrs Bates,' said Zoe with heavy patience, 'I'd be enormously grateful if you'd go and dust somewhere else. I'm busy.' The door was banged very hard behind Mrs Bates's departing form. With a grunt of laughter, Zoe spread her papers out, then began to go carefully through them. She was being overcautious, she knew, but it was important to her that Foster be pleased. Impressed, she substituted with a wry grin. She didn't want him to be merely satisfied, she wanted him to be really impressed. Amused by her behaviour, she returned her attention to her papers—until the vacuum cleaner started up just outside the door.

Setting her mouth in a tight line, her eyes hard, Zoe stared at the wall. I'm going to kill her, she thought mutinously. Making a determined effort to shut out the noise, desperately concentrating on her papers, she suddenly hurled her pen away when the vacuuming noise was accompanied by sporadic banging, as though the implement was being ruthlessly shoved against the skirting-board. Zoe dumped her papers on the sofa, got to her feet and marched over to the door. Flinging it open, she surveyed Mrs Bates with a glacial expression. Then she switched the vacuum cleaner off.

'Don't,' she said, between her teeth. 'I'm sure there are fourteen thousand other things you can do without trying to destroy the hall! Please go and do them.'

In answer, Mrs Bates gave her a look of dislike—and switched the vacuum cleaner back on. Desperately fighting the urge to wallop her, Zoe stepped over the lead, walked to the socket, wrenched the plug out and dropped it on the floor. Then she went into the study. Not bothering to close the door, or lower her voice, she said, slowly and with great feeling, 'She's doing it on purpose. Do you know that?' she asked reasonably. 'Do you? Are *you* persecuted by this woman? No, of course you're not. Only *I* am persecuted. First I have my hair dusted, then my back—should I proffer my feet for cleaning? Should I? And, as if that wasn't enough, when I ask her to desist, she rams the vacuum cleaner round the skirting-board, into the door... So I'm going to kill her, Foster. Now.'

With a snort of laughter, he got to his feet and walked across to close the door. 'She does her best,' he murmured, straight-faced.

'No, she doesn't,' she denied, beginning to see the funny side of it. 'She does her worst. To me, anyway. I don't even know why she doesn't like me! What did I ever do?'

'You came,' he said softly. 'She doesn't approve of you staying here with a single—er—gentleman.'

Giving a whoop of laughter, hastily stifled, her eyes gleamed at him over the hand she'd clamped across the mouth. 'Leading you astray, am I?'

'Oh, you'll never know,' he said, with such feeling that she had to bite her lip to stop her giggles.

'Want me to apologise?'

'It might make life more comfortable,' he agreed.

'You don't care if life's comfortable or not,' she derided.

'Don't I?' asked Foster softly.

'No! But, just to prove what a nicely brought-up young lady I am, I'll apologise to her. OK?'

'Thank you,' he said drily, with an ironic little inclination of his head.

Straightening her face, she walked back into the hall. 'Mrs Bates,' she began firmly, 'I owe you an apology.' When the severe face before her softened not one iota, Zoe gave a little sigh. 'It's not my place,' she continued hopefully, 'to criticise your work—and I'm not,' she added hastily, as the thin lips thinned further. 'It's just that I was trying to read some notes, for Mr Campbell,' she added, inspired, 'because he's so busy, and, well, I got a bit impatient. I'm sorry.' Unable to think of anything further to say to placate the blessed woman, she stared at her helplessly. With another long sigh, she murmured, 'Well, I'll—er—let you get on,' then hastily escaped into the sitting-room and closed the door before she became hysterical. Dratted woman. 'Come back, Laura, all is forgiven,' she whispered fervently.

Not five minutes later she heard the front door close. Rushing to the window, she watched in astonishment as Mrs Bates, hat very firmly jammed on her head, walked down the path. 'Good heavens,' she muttered.

'Quite,' Foster said softly from behind her.

Swinging round, she stared at him in amazement. 'She's gone. Did you tell her to leave?'

'No.'

'Then why?'

'Her time was up. She only agreed to work until six.' Looking at his watch, he added smoothly, 'It's exactly six now.'

'You little toad, why didn't you tell me before?'

'What, and miss all the fun?'

Shaking her head at him, she asked, 'Will she be back tomorrow?'

'Nope. Laura will be here. Said she was bored to tears. Cats, she said, make very poor conversationalists.'

Laughing, her good humour restored, Zoe shooed him out and went back to her papers. When she was satisfied that she'd covered all the points, she put the notes tidily away. There was nothing much to do now except wait for the report to come in from Meads. Which meant she'd be at a loose end again. Walking thoughtfully along to the study, she opened the door and poked her head inside.

'Got anything else for me to do?' she asked hopefully.

With a small smile, Foster reached across the desk, and picked up a piece of paper which he then handed to her. 'Rex Marston. Inventor, yachtsman, engineer. He's come up with a little gizmo to expedite sail furling. I know absolutely nothing about yachting.' A statement Zoe strongly doubted. However. 'On paper, it looks good. He wants backing to manufacture it. Find out all you can. If you like the look of it, invite him to dinner and we'll talk terms.'

'OK.' Clutching the paper to her, she gave

him a warm smile. 'Thanks. I'll start on it first thing in the morning.'

She liked Rex Marston. She also liked his wife. His ideas seemed feasible to her, his working demonstration of the gizmo, as Foster called it, impressive. Like Foster, she didn't know very much about sailing, so she set about extending her education. Chichester Yacht Club seemed a likely place to start. Yachtsmen, she found, liked to talk about their sport. Liked to expound at great length on this hull or that hull, this type of rigging, anchor, compass, whatever. They also seemed interested in the brief outline she gave of the gizmo. Would it sell? she wondered. Don't see why not, they answered.

So she invited Mr and Mrs Marston to dinner, and she found something else out, about herself. She liked playing hostess. Whether it was because the Marstons were exceptionally nice people, or because she had a talent for entertaining, she wasn't sure, but the evening went very smoothly, and she was glad to be able to pay Foster back, even if it was only in a small way. Also, Foster's confidence in her gave her own confidence a boost, especially when he agreed to back Rex Marston's little project.

Rex shook hands warmly with them both and then kissed Zoe warmly on the cheek. 'Thank you,' he whispered. 'I won't let you down.'

'I know you won't,' she murmured, smiling at him.

When they had left, and Foster had closed the front door, she remarked, 'They were a nice couple; I liked them.'

'So did I. If you married me, we could have many more such pleasant evenings.'

'So we could,' she mumbled evasively. 'I'd best go and check on the plants, I haven't given them a thought today,' and could have hit him at the knowing look he gave her, his eyes amused.

Collecting her jacket, she hurried out into the chilly night. The door of the greenhouse was wide open.

'Oh, knickers!' Inside she stared in dismay at the poor dying plants. All that hard work ruined. She should have felt like crying. Instead she was ashamed to admit that, after the first shock, she felt rather indifferent. Still, maybe she could save some. Unmindful of the navy patterned silk dress that Foster had insisted she buy for the dinner, she poked and prodded, in a rather sad attempt to find any plants worth rescuing. Perhaps they would revive, she thought, without much optimism. Giving them all a drink of water, she firmed the roots and, not knowing what else to do, wandered back to the house. Foster was at the back door watching her.

'Oh, dear,' he said wryly.

'Yeah. Someone left the greenhouse door open.'

'Someone?'

Not deigning to answer, she walked across to the sink to wash her grubby hands. As she reached for the towel, Foster captured one of her hands and stared down at the nails. The varnish she had so carefully applied before dinner was already chipped.

'I know, I know, nail varnish and potting sheds don't go very well together. Hardly an advertisement for hand cream, are they?'

'No.' Curling his fingers warmly round hers, he added humorously, 'If you married me I could take you away from all this drudgery.'

'Broken nails are hardly a basis for marriage,' she murmured awkwardly. 'Anyway, I told you that I wouldn't marry unless I was in love.'

'And you aren't.'

'No,' she said quietly.

'Is that final?' asked Foster softly, and she looked up, startled at the odd note in his voice. His face was quite still, the eyes expressionless, yet for a moment she had thought he sounded disappointed. He didn't *look* disappointed. He didn't look anything, yet suddenly she felt cold. She didn't want to marry him, she knew she didn't, so why this sense of disappointment at his intimation that he would not ask again?

'Yes,' she whispered.

'All right,' he said quietly. 'You get along to bed. I'm sorry about your plants, but thank you for helping to make the evening a success.'

Nodding, she went slowly and rather thoughtfully up to her room. Did she want to have her cake and eat it? she wondered, as she undressed. Many more such evenings, he'd said earlier. And she had enjoyed this one. Playing hostess for him. But it wouldn't always be like that. It couldn't.

It wasn't. She had a taste of the other side later that week. A very aggressive individual came knocking at the door, thrust rudely past the housekeeper and encountered Zoe on her way downstairs.

'All right, Laura,' she said quietly, 'I'll deal with it.' As soon as the housekeeper had gone back to the kitchen with a disapproving sniff, she continued down the stairs, giving herself a psychological advantage by remaining on the bottom step. 'Yes?' she asked, with an aloof little tilt of her head.

'Where's Campbell?'

'Who wants to know?'

'I want to bloody know!' stormed the man furiously, 'and don't tell me he's not bloody in, because I know damned well he is!'

'Did I say otherwise? And, if you want my co-operation, I suggest that you stop swearing at me,' said Zoe coldly.

'Where is he?' he demanded.

'Here,' Foster said softly from behind him. 'I don't recall that you had an appointment.'

'You know damned well I don't have an appointment!' The man swung round angrily. 'Neither do I intend to make one. What I have to say can be said here and now. You're an unscrupulous bastard, Campbell, and I give you fair warning that I won't take my dismissal lying down!'

'You may take it any way you choose,' Foster said coolly. 'Only you take it somewhere else.' Walking across to the front door, he opened it in silent invitation.

'Oh, no,' gritted the stranger, marching across with the intention of slamming it—only it didn't budge, nor did Foster look as though it was any effort to hold it against the other man's onslaught. With an angry grunt, the man allowed his hand to drop to his side. 'You can't dismiss me without good reason. There's tribunals...'

'So there are,' Foster said mildly. 'I suggest you go and see one.'

'I will! Don't think I won't. Ten years I managed that company!'

'Mismanaged,' Foster corrected.

'You never gave me a chance to do otherwise. Bought the company and dismissed me!'

'With a year's salary and a reference—and my patience is rapidly running out, Mr Taylor,' Foster continued in the same mild tone. 'Any further communications can be made through my solicitor, Manning and Webb in Chichester. Now, good day.'

Staring at Foster, a look of angry frustration on his face, Taylor said bitterly, 'I have a wife, kids...'

'Then I suggest you find a job more within your capabilities.'

'Oh, it's easy for you, isn't it? Well, I'm not leaving it there, and, believe me, Mr bloody high and mighty Campbell, you'll be sorry you ever heard of me . . .'

'Don't add stupidity to your errors. I don't take threats lightly.' With a little inclination of Foster's head, Ron Taylor, late of Freelings Office Furniture, was dismissed. For the second time in his career.

Closing the door, Foster turned to face Zoe. 'I'm sorry you had to witness such a distasteful display of bad manners.'

'Don't be pompous, Foster,' she said quietly. 'Did you dismiss him without good reason?'

'I never do anything without good reason.' Walking past her, he went back into his study.

She stared at the closed door, her mouth pursed. 'There endeth the first lesson,' she murmured to herself. She hoped that she never gave him cause to treat *her* in a like fashion. Walking across to the study, she pushed open the door.

'Don't,' he said softly.

'I wasn't going to,' she defended quietly.

'Good.'

'I merely came to ask if there was anything for me in the second post.'

'No. Were you expecting something?'

'Yes!' she said impatiently. 'A letter from the insurance company!'

'I'll give my lawyers a ring, get them to chase.'

'Thank you,' she said with mild sarcasm.

'My pleasure.'

'God, you're infuriating!' she muttered. Backing out, she closed the door with an angry little slam, marched out to the kitchen, collecting her jacket on the way, and told Laura she was going for a walk.

Kicking irritably at pebbles, Zoe walked down to the pub. In truth, she wasn't quite sure why she was so irritated with him. She'd known he had a temper, albeit a cold, calculating sort of one. And that, she told herself, had been a prime example of it. She thought that she'd rather be yelled at—and it only went to endorse her good sense in refusing to marry him. If she were to do so, that type of behaviour was something she could come to expect if she ever displeased him. Which she inevitably would, at some time or another. So why did she feel so damned disappointed?

Sitting at a corner table, she ignored the advances of a middle-aged man who seemed to think she had come to the pub for the express pleasure of his company. Eventually, when polite disclaimers didn't work, she told him in language he could understand. Not very ladylike, but what the hell—who wanted to be a lady all the time? As she sipped moodily at her drink, she decided that it was probably not a very auspicious time to ask Foster for something else to occupy her time. The two brief forays she'd made into business had whetted her appetite for more.

Another surprise was in store for her when she returned to the house. Foster's overnight bag was in the hall, and, as she closed the front door, he came lightly downstairs.

'Are you going away?' she asked surprised.

'Mm, for a day or two. Do you want Laura to sleep in the house?'

'No. I'm not nervous on my own. And I have the Major,' she said absently.

'OK. I'll probably be back Sunday night. Take care,' he said offhandedly.

Exchanging a bewildered glance with Laura as she came out from the kitchen, she murmured lamely, 'Bye...I didn't know he was going away,' she said to the housekeeper, as the front door closed with a rather nastily final sound.

'No more did I, dear. One minute he was shut in his study, the next packed and ready for the off. Don't let his right hand know what his left's doing, if you ask me. What would you like for dinner this evening?'

'Oh, anything,' she answered indifferently. 'Whatever.'

By Saturday evening she was bored to tears. Foster, despite his laconic ways, was at least a stimulating companion. The same could not be said of the Major. She missed him. Even if he didn't talk to her very much, he was usually there, and even to sit in silence with him was a great deal better than this. She should have been glad that she didn't even have to invent reasons for avoiding him, but she wasn't.

At eight o'clock she had a leisurely bath then spent some time on her poor raggedy nails. She hadn't even glanced into the greenhouse today, and, with a defiant little smile, she decided she didn't care. When she'd finished her nails, she wrapped herself in Foster's navy bathrobe and went down to watch television. Making herself a stiff gin and tonic, she lay on the sofa and idly watched an old film. It was the Major who alerted her. Long before she had heard the whisper of tyres on the drive, he was standing, head tilted expectantly, and she felt a swift rush of pleasure that Foster had come home early. As she heard his key in the front door, she went towards him, a smile of welcome on her face which slowly faded as she saw that he wasn't alone.

'Zoe, this is Adèle. Adèle, meet my house guest,' and both girls smiled politely at each other.

'Everything all right?' he asked Zoe.

'Sure, fine, couldn't be better.'

'Good. Adèle,' he murmured with his half-smile, 'please, sit down. What will you drink?'

'White wine, if you have it?' she said, giving Foster a wide smile. As he went out to get the wine from the room off the kitchen where he kept it, Zoe turned her attention to the other girl. She was slim, petite almost, with brown hair cut very short, gamine style. She also actually looked quite nice—and Zoe felt a distinct disinclination to be polite to her.

'Is it any good?' Adèle asked.

'What?'

'The film.' She smiled. 'I adore these old movies.'

'Oh, yes.'

'David told me about your fire. I'm so sorry, it must have been a terrible shock.'

'Yes.' At Zoe's curt answer, Adèle looked awkward and embarrassed, and Zoe felt a pig. Summoning up a smile, she apologised. 'Sorry, I'm not normally so rude. I was half asleep,' she lied, and added lamely, 'Hate being at a disadvantage.'

'Oh, that's all right,' said Adèle happily, obviously relieved there wasn't going to be a scene. 'I expect it's difficult for you when David brings someone home. Neither fish nor fowl, sort of thing.'

'Yes,' Zoe said thoughtfully, and couldn't quite make up her mind if Adèle's words had been a calculated dig, or were said in all innocence. 'Yes,' she repeated, 'it can be difficult.' It also seemed to imply that Foster brought home an army of women friends that Zoe was forced to be polite to. And why was Foster taking so long? she wondered sourly. So they could have a girlish chatter?

'Well, I think I'll toddle on up to bed, leave you in peace.'

'Oh, don't go yet,' Foster murmured, appearing with perfect timing which made Zoe wonder waspishly if he'd been hovering outside the door. She wouldn't have put it past him. 'I was hoping you'd give Adèle some hints on horticulture.'

'On what?' she asked in astonishment, swinging her legs to the floor and finishing off her drink in one quick swallow.

'Horticulture. Adèle is thinking of starting up her own nursery. I felt sure that you could give her some tips,' he said blandly.

With a sweet smile, Zoe plonked her glass on the mantelpiece. 'Really. What should I tell her? That it makes a hell of a mess of your nails?' Giving Adèle another lame smile, she sidled past Foster, and went up to her room. Now what game was he playing? Horticulture, indeed. She'd give him horticulture.

Unfortunately, he didn't give her a chance to give him anything. All of a sudden, he was very busy. Every time she tried to corner him he was just on the point of going out. Usually with Adèle. If Zoe went out, he was just coming in. If she came in, he went out. With Adèle. Except when she was in the nursery, when they would both appear, as though they'd been hovering in the vicinity waiting for her to make a move. She found it very irritating, not to say cross-making, and as a week slid by she became more and more short-tempered.

Adèle kept asking her questions she didn't know the answer to, about feeds, soil mix, which peat to use. What temperature for this plant, that plant. Why didn't she grow herbs?

Adèle asked kindly. Because she didn't know how! She knew what she'd like to grow. Poison ivy! Throughout it all, Foster wore his Cheshire Cat smile. The little dibber became a much abused tool. Zoe wished she could leave.

'Isn't there any news of the insurance money yet?' she asked him fractiously, when she finally managed to get him on his own.

'No. I told you, it takes time.'

'Time, time,' she muttered irritably. 'How much longer am I to go on living in limbo?'

'Is that what it is?' he asked gently. 'Are you so unhappy here?'

'No.' Heaving a big sigh, she stared at him awkwardly. She no longer felt comfortable in his presence and she didn't really know why. She was behaving like a spoilt child, and although her stupid behaviour angered her, she didn't seem able to to do anything about it. 'No,' she said again. 'I just feel unsettled, I suppose... I think I'll go out for the day. Maybe go and see Meg.'

'Why not go to Arundel?'

'Arundel? The castle, you mean?'

'Mm. It's a nice day. Quite spring-like. It'll do you good,' he said blandly.

'Will it?' she asked moodily. 'Oh, well, why not? How do I get there?'

She didn't find that Arundel did her any good at all. The castle was closed, and there weren't many shops of the sort that she could have pottered in to take her mind off Foster, and off Adèle. Anyone would think she was jealous, the way she was carrying on. Not liking herself very much, she wandered back towards the car park, across the river. Leaning her arms on the parapet of the bridge, she stared down into the river. She had to admit she'd been behaving very oddly of late. Ever since the fire, in fact. Could something like that radically change a person's personality? Or did it just make you more introspective? Feeling miserable, she turned to look at the castle. It really was lovely. Pity she wasn't in the mood to appreciate it. As she was about to walk on, she suddenly caught sight of Adèle, and frowned. Adèle was leaning against the ruined wall not fifty feet from where Zoe stood. She saw Adèle laugh and put out a hand. So she wasn't alone. Hating herself even more for her curiosity, Zoe edged nearer, wanting to know who she was with.

CHAPTER SIX

IT DIDN'T come as any great surprise to see that Adèle's companion was Foster, and, as he smiled at the other woman, Zoe curled her fingers tightly on the cold stone parapet. He never smiled at her like that. Never touched her face the way he was touching Adèle's. As he bent and brushed his mouth lightly across her cheek, swift pain stabbed through Zoe. A tight fist squeezed her heart. She was jealous, she thought blankly. She wanted to run down to them and scratch Adèle's eyes out. She'd never been jealous in her entire life, had thought herself incapable of such an emotion. Averting her gaze, she stared blindly down at her hands, at the white knuckles, and deliberately loosened her grip. To be jealous you had to desperately want or love—and love fiercely. And she wasn't in love with him, truly she wasn't, otherwise she would have agreed to marry him, wouldn't she? Hearing approaching footsteps, she turned her head away, not sure what might be reflected on her face.

'What?' Foster asked softly, coming to a halt beside her, and she gave a little start because she had thought he hadn't seen her.

'Nothing,' she mumbled, her face still averted.

'Fibber.'

Giving a ragged sigh, she turned to face him. 'Yes,' she whispered.

'But it's something not for sharing?' he asked gently.

'No.' Then, with a funny little shiver, she added, 'It's not important.'

'Mm.'

'Well, I'd best get back,' she said, attempting a bright smile which she knew must look like a grimace. 'The castle was closed,' she added stupidly. 'I didn't know that you were coming here.'

'No,' he said unhelpfully.

She stared at him, trying, she supposed, to see what was different, what had changed, but looked unhappily away when his face showed wry amusement. He knew, she thought. It was probably written all over her face. And, even if it wasn't, he'd probably have known. Very little escaped him; that was why he was so good at what he did.

'Jealous, Zoe?' he asked softly.

'No! No,' she said, more quietly.

'It isn't anything to be ashamed of...'

'I'm not ashamed, because I'm not jealous! Why should I be? And hadn't you better be getting back to Adèle? She'll wonder where you are.'

'She knows where I am—and what I'm doing,'

'And what are you doing?' she asked tartly, in an effort to disguise her pain.

'Trying to make you jealous,' he said simply, and she stared at him with her mouth open. 'Only if it hasn't worked...'

'You're *what*?'

Resting a hand either side of her on the parapet, effectively trapping her, he murmured very, very softly, 'Admit it. You were jealous as hell.'

'No.' When he lowered his head and peered intently into her eyes, she flushed and looked away.

'Jealousy isn't such a terrible thing, you know...'

'Isn't it?' she asked miserably.

'No. It doesn't mean you lose your identity,' he said gently, understanding her very well.

'No, but it's a sort of malicious god, isn't it? A destroyer.'

'Not necessarily—it doesn't have to be like that, Tiger,' and at the silly childhood name, she briefly closed her eyes that were suddenly pricking with tears.

'Doesn't it?'

'No.'

'Why did you want to make me jealous, Foster?' she asked, her voice barely audible, her eyes avoiding his.

'Why do you think?' he asked, his voice still gentle.

'I don't know,' she mumbled. 'Wanting to make me jealous implies that you care...'

'Go on,' he prompted.

'You—cared, is that it? And I didn't?'

'And?'

Her mind in turmoil, she fought to make sense of her racing thoughts. 'Is that what all those odd conversations were about?'

'Mm. I had to put the idea into your head, didn't I?' he asked softly. 'But not clarify it, or not until I was sure how you felt.'

'And you felt . . .' she began weakly.

'Yes.'

'But how? You barely knew . . .' Flicking her eyes up to his, she stared at him, and saw the truth there. 'You lied to me, didn't you? It wasn't because you recognised my name from the newscast on the fire, was it? You knew who I was all along.'

'Yes. Where you were, and who you were— always. I could have repaid the money any time over the last fifteen years.'

'Then why?'

'I was waiting for the right time,' he said simply.

'And that was it?'

'Yes.'

'But why?' she asked, confused.

'You know why.'

'I don't. How could I know?'

'Then I'll tell you.' Shifting his position slightly so that his arms were closer to her body, his thighs briefly touching hers, he began, 'I've wanted to have you around since you were seven years old. I wanted you when you were fifteen, eighteen, twenty. I've always wanted you. Only I had to wait. I'm very good at waiting. First I had to let you grow, find your feet, do all the things you wanted to do, try all the things you needed to try. Like me, you have a need to prove you can do things. So, I gave you space, time. Only once did I come close to stopping you, when you became engaged to Peter Fry... Only I decided that you would have the good sense to recognise it as a mistake—which you did.'

'That's terrible,' she whispered, horrified. 'Calculating.'

'I've always been calculating—you know that. Don't pretend to be shocked.'

'And if I hadn't had the sense to break off my engagement?' she queried faintly.

'I'd have broken it off for you. Think I couldn't have done?'

'No,' she sighed. She knew very well that he could have done. All those years knowing about her, stalking her—it was frightening. But she still didn't really understand why. 'Was that why you asked me to marry you? Because you wanted me?'

'Yes. Only Zoe Mitchell didn't believe in commitment, did she? She believed in a business partnership—so that was what I proposed—with fringe benefits,' he murmured, with that devastating half-smile, yet the eyes were watchful.

'But you didn't believe in lasting relationships. You said so,' she pointed out, frowning. 'You said...'

'I lied. So did you.'

'Not then,' she said hastily. 'I didn't know then . . .'

'No. But you do now, don't you? *Don't* you, Zoe?'

'Yes,' she whispered, an odd warmth sliding through her as he held her eyes with his own.

'You want me—as I want you. Now, this minute——' Tracing his thumb slowly along her lower lip, he said throatily, 'I want to touch you the way a man touches a woman. I want to undress you slowly, trail my mouth from your eyes to your toes. I want to enter you, be a part of you——' and there was a funny little growl in his voice, a sheen of perspiration on his forehead. 'How shocked do you think people would be if I laid you across one of those benches beside the river and made love to you? Slowly, with infinite care, infinite enjoyment. If I caressed you the way I've wanted to caress you, said all the things I've wanted to say—and couldn't, because you didn't know how I felt . . .'

'Oh, God,' she croaked huskily.

'Yes.' Moving his hand round to her nape, he slid his fingers into her thick hair, his eyes on her mouth. 'I want to slide my tongue between your teeth, I want to touch my body to yours, like this, and this,' he muttered thickly, shifting slightly to emphasise his words, making her aware of his arousal. 'I want . . .'

'I want to go home,' she groaned, her body melting against his.

'Yes... You will drive home very, very slowly. Very, very carefully. I'll take Adèle home and meet you there...'

Adèle. God, she'd forgotten Adèle! Turning her head, she looked for the other girl.

'She's waiting in my car,' he said softly, reading her thoughts very accurately.

'But...'

'In return for the chance to run the nursery,' he murmured throatily, as her startled eyes flew back to his, 'she agreed to a little deception. Adèle means nothing to me. Nor I to her.'

'The nursery? But I run the nursery.'

'No, you don't. You're much better as a business associate. Aren't you?'

'Am I?'

'Yes. Now go home.' Turning, he walked quickly away, leaving Zoe to stare bemusedly after him. When he was out of sight she turned slowly and began to walk shakily back to her car, her thoughts in turmoil. There wasn't any doubt that she would drive home slowly. She had to; her concentration was shot to pieces, but she arrived safely.

With a nervous, sick excitement, she showered and wrapped herself in a towelling robe, then meandered slowly through the house. The Major, picking up her unsettled state of mind, padded softly after her. As the minutes ticked past, became an hour, her excitement turned to fear—and then to anger. Anger was easier to cope with. Where the hell was he? The way he'd spoken... As though he couldn't wait... She refused to consider that he might have had an accident. She ran back upstairs, dragged on jeans and sweatshirt, and stormed out to the greenhouse. Stabbing at plants that most certainly didn't need, or deserve, stabbing, she listened for Foster's car. In the event, muttering furiously, fearfully, to herself, she didn't hear him return. The first intimation she had of his presence was the cool draught on her back as the greenhouse door opened.

Spinning round, she glared at him.

'Ask me where I've been,' he commanded softly.

'No. I don't care where you've been.'

'Then ask me why I took so long.'

'I don't care about that, either.'

'Then why are you in a temper?'

'I'm not in a temper! I'm catching up on my potting because someone gave the rights away behind my back, and I want to leave it all shipshape!'

With a soft laugh, he walked across and removed the small dibber from her hand, then tossed it negligently on to the bench. 'You're an appalling liar, Zoe Mitchell.' Taking her hand, he examined it for a moment, brushed the grains of soil from her palm and then pressed a warm kiss on it, his eyes holding hers.

'I had a puncture...so simple, and quite infuriating. Come.'

With a shaky sigh, she took his outstretched hand. They walked towards the house in silence. Upstairs, and into his room. 'Come and shower me,' he said softly.

'Oh, God.' She felt like a schoolgirl, unsure, bewildered, excited. Her breath erratic, her heart beating unevenly, she allowed him to lead her into the bathroom. The door was closed very softly behind them. His eyes on hers, he began to strip. His shoes, his sweater, his trousers, socks, and finally his pants. 'You'll get your clothes wet,' he murmured—and his eyes looked black, pupil and iris merged.

With trembling hands, she tugged her sweater over her head before belatedly remembering that she had no bra on, and started to turn her back. His soft 'No' halted her. Keeping her eyes lowered, she stepped out of her jeans, then hesitated before removing her pants.

'Please,' he said softly. Blindly taking his hand again, she walked with him into the small shower cubicle. It was only intended for one. There was no way that she could avoid touching him, her body met his from knee to hip to chest. His hands remained by his sides, his eyes still on hers, but his body responded to her nearness and she gave a little moan, deep in her throat. Lifting one hand, he moved the shower head lower so that it wouldn't soak her hair, then turned it on. He handed her the soap, and waited, his eyes black, the pupil enlarged as fine spray slicked their bodies. It was the most erotic thing she had ever experienced.

'If I drop it,' she said shakily, 'there won't even be room to pick it up.'

'No. So don't drop it... Foot first,' he said quietly, raising one knee so that she could reach, which brought him even closer.

Soaping his foot, calf, shin, knee, her eyes on her task, she gave shaky little gasps for breath as he touched against her, as he shifted, moved, offered the other foot, tantalised, tormented her until she was shaking so badly that she couldn't continue. Wordlessly offering the soap, she closed her eyes as he began to soap her. Her shoulders, gently kneading out the tension, arms, wrists, hands. Her sides to her waist, then up over her bust, his hands lingering, touching, massaging. Then her stomach, pelvis, groin, and another little moan escaped her.

'Over-rated, Zoe?' he sighed, his mouth touching hers fleetingly, but his breathing was too ragged, which gave her the courage to open her eyes. Steam had misted his hair, eyebrows, face, and she arched helplessly against him as his hands moved to her back, to her buttocks. 'Oh, Foster, I think I'm going to faint.'

'Not yet. Later,' he said thickly.

'I don't think I'll last till later,' she whispered, and even the water on her lips tasted erotic. Without even thinking about it, her hands moved to his body, smoothed his back, touched his waist, buttocks, moved to linger on his thighs, then, with a deep shuddering breath, touched his manhood and the world revolved crazily. She barely remembered the shower being turned off, being wrapped in a thick towel and carried into the bedroom. Her eyes closed, she reached for him blindly, pulled him towards her, wrapped her legs round him, held him tight—and died a thousand times as he made love to her. An exquisite torture. Slowly, refusing to be rushed, he roused her again and again until finally, unable to hold back any longer, he took her to the ultimate peak.

'Still think it was over-rated?' he asked huskily, his breathing as erratic as her own.

'No,' she whispered. Opening her eyes, she stared into his strong face. There was no arrogance now, only a look of gentleness, tenderness. His hair was wildly tangled, and she put up a shaky hand to push it back off his forehead. 'It obviously depends who you do it with ... Is it ...?'

'No,' he said softly, 'it isn't.'

'You don't know what I was going to say,' she protested weakly.

'Yes, I do. You were going to ask if it was always like that for me, with other women, weren't you?'

'Well, is it?' she asked tartly.

'No.'

'Not even the teensiest bit?'

'No.'

'Good. I must be pretty special, then, hm?'

With a little grunt of laughter, he dropped a kiss on her nose. 'Pretty damned special, yes. Now will you marry me?' he asked softly—and for a moment, just a fleeting moment, she thought he looked unsure, but then he grinned and the moment was lost.

'It's really what you want?'

'Yes.'

'Then I will,' she said simply, and he gave a long sigh, his eyes briefly closing. With another funny little sigh, he rolled to his feet and walked across to his dressing-table. From the drawer he took a small box, and walked back to the bed. Perching on the edge of the mattress, he placed the box squarely on her navel.

With a trembling hand she opened it, and gave a little gasp of pleasure. 'Oh, Foster!' Taking out the ring, she held it to the light so that the diamonds winked and glittered. One large diamond, set about with seven smaller ones.

'Like it?'

'Oh, yes,' she whispered. 'It's beautiful.' And wildly expensive, she thought with a sudden inward qualm. She thought she'd be terrified of losing it. Taking it from her, he slid it on to her ring finger. It was only very slightly loose.

'We can have it made smaller tomorrow.' Lifting her hand, he kissed it softly. 'How soon will you marry me, Zoe?'

Looking at him, seeing how serious he was, she found herself saying, 'As soon as it can be arranged.' They had no reason to delay, she supposed, and she did want to marry him, didn't she?

As though aware that she might be having doubts, he leaned forward and kissed her. Rolling back on to the bed, he pulled her into his arms. 'I don't think I'll be able to keep my hands off you,' he warned, bending to nibble her ear. 'Waiting for you taxed me to the limit.'

With a long sigh, she snuggled into his embrace, her mouth seeking the warm pulse that beat in his throat. 'I'm finding this almost impossible to believe,' she confided. 'It seems odd, somehow, and a little bit frightening. Childhood friends, and now lovers.'

'And soon to be husband and wife,' he added raising his head to smile at her.

'Yes... And I barely know the first thing about you, do I? Fill in the gaps for me, Foster. Tell me about you, the real you, not the man you've been pretending to be since I came to stay.'

'I've not been pretending,' he denied. 'Just keeping myself in check, I suppose.' With an odd little shrug, he put the pillows against the headboard and levered them both up, his arm warmly round her, the quilt dragged over their legs.

'Go on, begin at the beginning, when you left with my savings,' she prompted.

'Mm.' Settling himself more comfortably, holding her hand in his, resting them both on his powerful thigh, he began slowly, 'I went to

London. Caught a train to Charing Cross—and then just wandered, I suppose. I exchanged my suitcase for a rucksack because it was easier to carry, lived rough for a few days until I'd found my way around, listened, learnt. Got a tiny room in a run-down boarding-house in Battersea, did odd jobs for the—woman—who ran it,' and a rather cynical smile fleetingly touched his mouth. What sort of odd jobs, she wondered? And the thought must have shown on her face because his smile altered, became amused. 'Not those sort of jobs, *odd* jobs, as in mending, sweeping up, making beds. I did them in lieu of rent.' But could he have done other things in lieu of rent? He'd been a very attractive boy. Even at fifteen, he'd looked older, mature.

'Was she...'

'A prostitute? Yes. Eventually, three of them took up residence in the house and I did odd jobs for all of them. Ran errands, bought the gin.' Another small smile. 'Actually, they were very nice to me, treated me like a kid brother. Gave me some very good advice on how to survive in the capital, how to be streetwise... I got to know street traders, bookies, loan sharks. I got a job as a messenger for a travel company—cheap clothes don't matter so much when you have a uniform to cover them. From there I became a messenger for an insurance company, then for a bank, and eventually, where I wanted to be, internal messenger for a firm of merchant bankers. That's where the money is—and that's what I wanted to learn. How to make it. I learnt about stock markets, shares, gilts. For two years I absorbed information like a sponge. I began to buy good clothes. A little at a time—save up, get something good, something that would last. I moved to better lodgings, and I put into practice the laws of supply and demand.'

'How?' she asked, fascinated.

With a self-deprecating smile, he explained, 'You buy something, anything, or know where you can always pick it up—it doesn't really matter what it is, all you have to do is persuade people that they need it. Advertise. "Wanted" columns in the paper. Two, maybe three. You know the sort of thing, you must have seen them: "Urgently wanted, such and such"—and then you put in an advertisement selling it, "Going cheap", etc.'

'And the people who've seen the "Wanted" ads, and the "For Sale" ads——'

'Yes, think they'll make a quick buck. And they do, mostly. There are a lot of people who live entirely like that. From newspapers. They don't need an expensive office, or overheads. You use box numbers. There's always someone who will buy...'

'And then, when they try to sell it back, you no longer want it?'

'Mm. But it takes time—and I was in a hurry. When I'd accumulated some cash, I opened a bank account. Studied the markets, what held its price, what was likely to go up... I found myself a broker and, cautiously at first, began to play the stock market. I began buying larger articles, selling for a higher profit. Bought a run-down house, did it up evenings and weekends, sold it. Bought another. By the time I was twenty-two, I owned quite a lot of property, some land, had a healthy bank balance.'

'You make it sound easy. But it wasn't, was it?'

'No, Tiger, not easy in terms of time, hard work, but when you're doing it for yourself it makes a hell of a difference, and hard work never bothered me. I made some mistakes, but never the same mistake twice. I had a flat in Belgravia, a woman friend who thought she was set up for life...'

'A mistake on her part,' she remarked drily.

'Mm.'

'How old was she?'

'Twenty-eight.'

'Toy boy,' she teased.

'Mm, but not now,' he said softly, pushing himself down the bed and pulling her down to join him so that she was trapped beneath him.

'No, not now,' she echoed breathlessly. Sliding her arms round his warm back, she raised her face for his kiss. 'And now you're established, have a reputation, power.'

'Mm.'

'And how do you keep this terrific body in such good shape?' she asked softly, her fingers touching against the hard-packed muscle in his back.

'Squash, skiing, when I have time, making love to a beautiful witch with black hair and blue eyes—who, incidentally, talks too much.'

Smiling, she stopped talking.

Over the next few days she came to see a different side of him. A warm, gentle, fun side. Quiet still, but softer, mellow almost, and, like him, she found it almost impossible to keep her hands to herself. From being a non-toucher, she became a toucher. Each time they met her hands would go out to him, and even his amused little smiles warmed her. From seeing very little of him, she was now very rarely out of his company. He indulged her childish desire to walk on walls, jump puddles—reverting to childhood, he called it, yet it didn't deter him from boyish acts of showing off, jumping railings she couldn't jump, doing fifty press-ups to her two. They did a lot of laughing, and a lot of loving, yet always in the back of her mind was the feeling, not of dissatisfaction exactly, but of unease. She couldn't quite get rid of the suspicion of manipulation, or quite forget how he had stalked her. Mostly she managed to push the doubts aside, but sometimes, usually at night, like now, as she lay awake in the big bed with Foster asleep beside her, they would return to trouble her.

Easing herself up gently, so as not to disturb him, Zoe sat with her back against the headboard and watched him. Watched the slow rise and fall of his chest, the tidy way he slept. No tangling in the covers for him, she thought with a small smile. He lay straight, like a knight on a stone tomb, one arm across his chest, the other by his side. In fact, not unlike a knight at all, she thought fancifully, with that straight, arrogant nose, the controlled mouth, and then she shivered as she recalled the way that same mouth touched her. Unable to help herself, she put out her hand and trailed her finger across his lower lip, then grinned as he twitched. She wanted to cuddle up close to him, feel his warm flesh against hers, feel his body respond to her nearness. And yet. Maybe she was just being foolish. He always seemed eager for her company. Eager to be with her, and to surprise her. With a little sigh, she snuggled back under the covers and slid one arm across him to hold him close. Dropping a light kiss on his shoulder, she closed her eyes.

The next morning, as they were having breakfast, he surprised her yet again. Laying his knife and fork tidily on his plate, he leaned back in his chair, and watched her for a few moments in silence before suddenly saying, 'Come to Rome with me.'

'Rome?' she asked blankly, her fork suspended half-way to her mouth.

'Mm. You got your passport back, didn't you?'

'Yes.'

'Then there's no reason why you shouldn't come. Is there?' he asked softly.

'No... When are you going?'

'This afternoon.'

'Foster!'

'What?' he asked innocently.

'You know very well what! Don't give much notice, do you?'

'How much notice do you need? Just throw a few things in a case—anything you haven't got we can buy there.'

'Well, isn't that just typical of a man? I have to wash my hair, make sure I have clean undies, oh, a hundred and one things. How long are we going for?'

'A few days, two, three.'

Staring at him, she shook her head helplessly. 'What time's the flight?'

'One-thirty...'

'One-thirty? But that means we'll have to leave here at—where from? Gatwick? Heathrow?'

'Just be ready by twelve, OK?' Giving her an infuriating smile, he poured himself a cup of tea.

'What a dictator you are.' She stared at him in exasperation.

'And don't you just love it,' taunted Foster.

'No, I don't.'

'Liar.'

'Nothing of the sort,' she said loftily. 'The only reason I'm allowing it this time is because I want to go to Rome. Had you been going to Southend, I would have refused.'

'Mm.'

'I don't like being manipulated.'

'You liked it in bed this morning,' he pointed out smugly. 'Didn't you?'

'That was entirely different.'

'Nice though, hm?'

'Go away.'

Finishing his tea, he got to his feet, gave her an amused smile, and walked off whistling. She threw her napkin at him. Wretch. Slowly finishing her meal, she tried to be practical, but his nonchalant air was infectious. What the hell—anything she forgot, she could buy there... She gave a small grin. Hadn't taken her long to get used to having money, had it?

'And what are the pair of you looking so pleased about?' Laura asked, coming in to clear the table. 'I've just met David with a broad grin on his face.'

'He's been manipulating me,' answered Zoe, unable to keep her own grin in check.

'And don't you just love it!' Laura laughed.

'Oh, don't you start. Did he tell you? We're off to Rome for a couple of days.'

'And you don't want to go?' asked Laura in disbelief.

'Oh, yes, I do. I was just trying to knock some of that horrid complacency out of him.'

'Did you succeed?'

'No.'

'No,' Laura echoed with a smile. 'He's been used to having his own way too long. But he's happy, isn't he? I don't think I'd ever heard him laugh until you came—and I always thought that rather sad. Now he's like a dog with two tails.'

'Is he?' asked Zoe, pleased and gratified. 'I hope so.' Getting to her feet, she gave the housekeeper a warm smile. 'I'd best go and pack, wash my hair, we've to be away by twelve.'

'Plenty of time, it's only just gone nine. Give me a shout if you need anything.'

'I will. Thanks, Laura.'

Fiumicino airport was some way from the city, and Zoe happily window-gazed. Flat fields slowly gave way to industrial areas, wide busy streets whose beautiful names she recited to herself like a litany, Portuense, Viale, Trastevere. Then across the Tiber, the bridges in her imagination looking much as they must always have done, and then, before her senses could adjust, they entered the old part of the town—ancient Rome, and she exclaimed delightedly. It was so old, so exactly as it should have been—so exactly as the mind might conjure it up. The Colosseum, a ruined amphitheatre, rising tier on tier, magnificent in ruin. The only sour note was the presence of the tourist coaches, and Zoe had a selfish desire for them to be gone so that she could have the

place to herself, soak up the atmosphere un-
hindered by tourists.

'Can we stop?' she asked wistfully, turning
to peer out of the rear window in an effort not
to miss anything.

'Sure.' Foster threw a few quick words to the
driver, in fluent Italian which made Zoe look
at him speculatively, and the cab pulled in to
the kerb with a total disregard for anyone following or trying to cross the road.

'Rome traffic is some of the worst in the
world,' Foster pointed out drily. 'I defy anyone
to find a car that hasn't a scrape or a dent. A
pedestrian who hasn't, at some time or another,
been nearly maimed. Don't take any notice of
pedestrian crossings—despite signs telling you
to advance, don't: you're liable to get run over.
Motorists just ignore them.'

'Obviously you're an old hand at this,' she
commented with a little grin. 'I was most impressed by the fluent Italian.'

'A mere trifle,' he grinned.

'How many languages do you speak, for
goodness' sake?'

'Oh,' then with a teasing, sideways glance at
her, he admitted, 'Five.'

'Huh, show-off.'

Laughing, he took her arm in a comforting
grip, and led her across the busy road to the
Colosseum. 'Most of the ruins,' he continued
in a lofty, informative tone, 'weren't caused by
age or time, as you might think, but because
ancient Roman vandals filched building blocks

and pillars from each other for their own structures or to build something else,' and Zoe had a crazy image of leather-skirted Romans, with sandal-shod feet, creeping out at dead of night to rob a nearby building, only to have the same thing happen to themselves a few nights later.

'I bet they were never buildings at all,' she laughed, 'I bet no one ever finished them.'

'Quite possibly. It's an intriguing thought.'

As he escorted her towards the great arena of the Colosseum, she gave a little sigh. Here Christians had fought for their lives against lions that were probably as bewildered as themselves; here well-born Romans had watched, indifferent to the fate of their fellow man, intent only on the sport.

'It's awesome, isn't it? As though it all happened yesterday.'

'Mm, even the lifts that brought the Christians up to be slaughtered still work,' he murmured. 'Their technology was truly remarkable—you can just about make out where they are, in the centre of the arena. And up there,' he continued pointing, 'the nobles sat, no doubt laying wagers on the length of time it would take one of the lions to kill.'

'You can almost hear the cries, can't you? The roars,' and she shivered suddenly as though someone had just walked over her grave. 'And yet, are we any more civilised now?' she murmured, almost to herself, thinking of terrorists, hijackers.

'No, just a better façade. Come along, it will be dark soon.'

Turning to give him a smile, she tucked her hand through his arm. 'Ancient history not your scene, my friend?'

'No,' he smiled. 'But I didn't mean to dampen your enthusiasm. As you are no doubt beginning to discover, I have no soul.'

'But beautiful eyes—and a terrific mouth,' she whispered, planting a kiss on his lower lip. 'That more than makes up for having no soul.' With another smile, she turned to retrace her steps.

The taxi-driver, obviously taking advantage of the fact that he had tourists in the cab, drove them the long way round. Not that Zoe would have known, but Foster was familiar with Rome and seemed to think it amusing, which she doubted he would have done if she hadn't been in the cab with him. But to Zoe it was all new and exciting, and she was trying to see everything at once, until Foster promised. 'We'll take a day to look round before we leave, OK?'

'Yes, thank you,' she said, giving his hand a tight squeeze. 'I didn't even ask why we were here, did I? Presumably you have some business to attend to?'

'Mm. I'm on the board of a company that owns several restaurants here. Their profits are down, and I want to know why. So I'll attend their board meeting tomorrow—I don't like losing money.'

'No, well, you wouldn't, would you?' she teased. 'Especially now when you're about to acquire an expensive wife.'

'Are you going to be expensive, Zoe?' he asked softly, and she shook her head, her eyes laughing at him.

'Only in the amount of your time I'm going to take up.'

'Promise?' he demanded, and she felt that lovely warmth spread through her insides.

'Promise,' she echoed huskily.

Their hotel was tucked away in a little side-street off the Via Veneto; they were booked into a double room and Zoe gave Foster a wry glance. Not that the man at Reception showed any interest, his face remaining impassive. But then, no doubt, he had seen it all before.

'I refuse to creep along the corridor at dead of night for the pleasure of your company,' Foster asserted, once they were alone in their room.

'The pleasure of my body, you mean.'

'Yes. It isn't a pleasure I wish to relinquish, even for a few days. The sooner we're married, the better—I find I want my brand on you. Think I didn't see the glances you've been getting, ever since we landed?'

'Just a natural appreciation of beauty,' answered Zoe loftily, walking across to bounce on one of the beds. 'Think we'll both fit into a single?' she asked softly.

'Yes.' Stripping off his jacket and tie, he kicked off his shoes and joined her. 'We'll just have to lie very close together,' he murmured against her neck. 'But, first, I think we ought to try out the shower, make sure it's big enough.'

With a gurgle of laughter, she shoved him on to the floor.

By the time they'd finished the rather lengthy shower and dressed, Zoe was impatient to go out and explore. 'We have so little time,' she wailed, 'and I might never come again.'

With an indulgent smile, Foster put his wallet in the back pocket of his trousers and firmly buttoned the flap. 'Unfortunately,' he explained wryly, 'beautiful as Rome is, it also has an inordinate number of pickpockets.' Shrugging into his jacket and checking that he had the key, he escorted her back downstairs.

'Can we sit out at a pavement café? Eat spaghetti? Watch the world go by?'

'Mm, hm. Will you be warm enough?' he asked softly, pulling her to him by the lapels of her leather jacket and rubbing his nose gently against hers.

'We-ell, I might need your arm round me...'

Laughing, he pushed her out into the street, then captured her hand in his and tugged her down the hill and along twisting little side-streets, not even allowing her to look in the shops they passed.

'Why are we in such a hurry?' she asked breathlessly.

'Because I'm starving, because I want to show you the Spanish Steps, the Trevi Fountain, and then I want to huddle with you on the dark forecourt of a little café I know, where you can make a mess with spaghetti, drink good wine, and watch the stars. All right?'

'Oh, yes, lovely,' she responded, hugging warmly against his arm.

The Spanish Steps were a sad disappointment. She had somehow expected them to be more impressive, not that she would have dreamt of saying so to Foster, although her expressive little sigh probably said it all for her. The Trevi Fountain was much more the thing, although she had somehow not expected it to be huddled in the middle of shops and cafés. It barely had room to breathe. Foster handed her some coins and, with a little smile, she tossed them into the floodlit water. Leaning her arms on the wide rim, she peered in, hoping to see them drift to the bottom.

'Did you make a wish?' he teased.

'Of course... Where next?'

'Food,' he said, laughing.

The spaghetti turned out to be excellent, the wine—of which Zoe freely confessed she drank too much—was potent, and the walk back to the hotel was a far more leisurely affair than the walk down had been.

'Drunkard,' taunted Foster as she stumbled slightly on the uneven pavements.

'Not so,' she denied. 'I just have heightened perceptions. And don't think that I don't know why you plied me with so much wine...'

'Aw, shucks, does that mean I won't get to have my wicked way with you?'

'Er, no, it probably means the wicked way will be more uninhibited than usual.'

'Then can we hurry up before these inhibitions return?'

Laughing, she quickened her pace towards the hotel. They were still laughing when they erupted into their room, and Foster pulled her into his arms and kissed her hard. 'If I put the heater on, we won't need any covers, will we?' he asked, gently rubbing his mouth across hers.

'No.' While he walked across the room to turn the heater on, she went to the window.

'Don't close the shutters,' he murmured, capturing her hand and holding it against his cheek.

'All right,' she whispered.

'I feel like being totally chauvinistic,' he continued softly. 'I want to lie on the bed and watch you undress, and then I want you to make love to me.'

Her insides liquefying, she nodded, and when he was lying naked on the narrow bed she slowly undressed, standing in the shaft of moonlight that filtered through the un-shuttered window.

'God, you're beautiful,' he said thickly.

'So are you,' she whispered drily, as she allowed her eyes to run over his magnificent

body. Walking towards the bed, her move-
ments slow, lethargic, she knelt beside him and
ran her palm down his chest, over his flat
stomach, and then halted, her breath lodging
in her throat. 'Oh, Foster,' she breathed, sitting
back on her heels, then, bending so that her
soft hair brushed against him, she trailed her
mouth across his flat stomach, into the hollows
formed by his hips, deliberately tantalising both
him and herself until her body was shaking with
the effort to maintain control. With a groan,
he grasped her shoulders and hauled her up to
lie on top of him, his mouth capturing hers in
a kiss that was almost savage in its intensity.
Her heart beating erratically against his, she
fitted herself to him, her knees drawn up either
side of his thighs. Pushing her hands into his
thick hair, she returned his plundering kisses
with equal urgency while her body moved with
the exquisite rhythm that was as old as time.

CHAPTER SEVEN

WHEN Zoe woke in the morning, she was clasped warmly in Foster's arms, her head resting on his shoulder. Mumbling sleepily, she pressed a soft kiss on his chin, then moved her hand up to rub against the scratchy bristles. Lifting her eyes to his, she smiled. 'Good morning. I just love Rome, don't you?'

With a slow lazy smile that turned her heart over, he murmured, 'Oh, yes, especially the nights. You are one very incredible lady, do you know that?' Then he laughed softly when she blushed. Moving his warm body suggestively against hers until she could feel his arousal, she groaned weakly as she felt her body respond.

'What time do you have to be at your meeting?'

'Unfortunately, far too soon.' Pressing a swift, hard kiss on her mouth, he rolled easily to his feet and padded into the bathroom.

Hoisting herself up, she smiled to herself, and, climbing more slowly out, she followed him.

As she put the finishing touches to her make-up, she watched him through the mirror as he fixed his cuff-links. The dark grey suit fitted him to perfection, as did all his clothes, whether they were casual or formal. His black shoes were polished to a high shine, his white shirt crisp, the tie plain grey, a fraction lighter than his suit. His face was controlled, serious—and for a moment he seemed like a remote stranger, not at all like the man who had tickled her in the shower not fifteen minutes previously until she had begged for mercy. And then he looked up, caught her eye, and grinned. He really was beautiful, she thought—she could understand his need to brand her; it was the way she felt herself. My property, keep off.

'You don't have to attend it, if you don't want to,' he told her, flicking an imaginary speck of dust off his sleeve.

'I want to,' she said quietly. 'I long to see you in action. I bet you're a formidable opponent. Will it all be conducted in Italian?'

'No. In English—they think I don't understand the language.'

'Ah, so when they mutter among themselves, thinking you won't understand a word of it . . .'

'Mm. Ready?'

'As I'll ever be. They won't mind me coming?' and, at the wry look he gave her, she grinned. 'They don't get a choice, huh?' Amused, she accompanied him downstairs.

The board meeting went exactly as she had expected it would. Foster would have made a brilliant poker player. The other three members of the board, who had greeted her so warmly and with what seemed genuine pleasure, slowly wilted before Foster's concise onslaught. What had they done to rectify the situation? Why not? Had they personally inspected each restaurant? Interviewed the staff? And on and on, until, only an hour after the meeting started, Foster brought it to a conclusion.

'They will now personally inspect each and every restaurant, kitchen, table and chair,' she murmured wryly, feeling quite sorry for the poor men left behind. 'Interview every staff member from the head waiter to the cleaner...'

'They'd better,' he said grimly. 'Talk about mismanagement. What a bloody waste of time...' Clearly making an effort to throw off his irritation, he gave her a small smile. 'Want to go and inspect the Vatican?'

'Please...I could go on my own if you want to do something else...' she offered tentatively.

'Let you loose on the male population of Italy?' he asked in mock outrage. 'My God, woman, have some sense.'

Gurgling with laughter, she hugged his arm. 'Just a thought. You have no need to stay now, do you?'

'No, but just to prove how indulgent I can be, after the Vatican, we'll make a whistle-stop tour of Rome, have a quick look at the shops—Gucci included, which is not far from the fountain...'

'Don't I get fed?'

'Fed? Oh, well, what the hell, in for a penny...'

They flew back on the late flight, arriving home well after midnight. Tired and happy, she curled against his strong back in the wide bed, her mind still whirling with the images of the past day. Any doubts that she had harboured about their marriage were now dispelled. She loved him, and he had more than proved that he was happy in her company. A smile on her face, she drifted into sleep.

Foster was already up and dressed when she woke, having probably already spent a few industrious hours in his study, she thought wryly. When she joined him for breakfast, he looked pointedly at his watch. 'You have no stamina, Miss Mitchell. I have been up since six-thirty.'

'Bully for you. Pass me the marmalade.'

'Please.'

Poking her tongue out at him, she wound her leg round his under the table and gently massaged his calf with her toes. 'I'll take the Major out for a nice brisk walk—that'll set me up for the day.'

'In that case I'll come with you. Seeing you set up for the day is a definite must on anyone's itinerary.'

Laughing, she said, 'It's your own fault—you shouldn't be such an ardent lover.'

'Are you complaining?' he asked softly.

'No.'

As soon as she'd finished eating, she went to get her jacket. It looked as though it was going to rain. Again. They wandered through the woods, allowing the Major to run where he would, Zoe's hand tucked into Foster's pocket, neither of them caring about the rain or the dripping trees. They idly discussed the wedding, details of which Foster was waiting to hear from the registrar, debated her need for an outfit, and whether they should invite her mother. In truth, she was quite happy for it to remain private. Selfish of her, but she didn't honestly think that her mother would mind, since she had her own family now in the States.

When they returned, entered by the back door, still hand in hand, their hair damp from the misty rain, Foster grabbed the dog's collar as he began to walk across Laura's immaculate floor. 'Sit!'

With a look of injured innocence, the Major sat. Taking the dog's towel from under the sink, Zoe handed it to Foster with a small grin. Before she could do anything about the mud that she had now tracked across the kitchen floor, she heard the phone in his study begin to ring. 'OK, I'll get it.' Kicking off her muddy shoes, she padded through to the study.

'Hello? Oh, hello, Mr McKinley, I don't suppose there's any news yet, is there?' and then she felt her heart begin to race as she took in what he was saying. 'When?' she demanded. 'Yes, no, I expect he forgot...' As Foster walked slowly into the room, she stared at him blankly, the telephone in her hand forgotten.

Walking across to her, he took the receiver from her lax grasp, and replaced it carefully on its rest. His expression was impossible to read.

'It was Mr McKinley,' she murmured, her wide eyes fixed on his face. 'He said the insurance money had been paid two weeks ago.'

'Yes.'

'But you didn't tell me...'

'No.'

'Why? Why didn't you tell me?' she asked in bewilderment. When he didn't immediately answer, she ran one hand distractedly through her damp hair, as she tried to make sense out of it. 'I don't understand. You knew how important the money was to me. Why didn't you tell me?'

His dark eyes empty, he stared back at her, then shoving his hands into his jeans pocket, he leaned back against the desk. 'Because I wanted you to stay,' he admitted quietly. 'If I'd given you the money, you might have left.'

'But I'd agreed to stay, agreed to marry you...'

'Not then you hadn't.'

'But why not tell me later? Foster, you can't just take someone's money and not tell them. It's theft,' she said weakly. 'Deceit...'

'Yes.'

He didn't even look ashamed, she thought dazedly. Not uncomfortable, not guilty. Did he think she wouldn't mind? she wondered incredulously. Did he think she would just accept the misappropriation of her money? 'Did *you* need the money? Was that it?'

'Would you have lent it to me if I had?'

'Yes, of course I would. *Did* you need it?'

'No. Funny, I never thought of that.'

'Foster, I . . .' But the sudden shrilling of the telephone made her break off in mid-sentence. As Foster picked it up and turned his back, she walked slowly out. She needed to think.

Unable to fully grasp what had happened, she walked along the hall and out of the front door. Wandering aimlessly along the lane, she felt numb. Her hands pushed into her jacket pockets, her head down, she scuffed along the road, seeing nothing, hearing nothing, unaware that the rain was heavier. Why? her mind kept repeating. Why would he do such a thing? So that she would stay, he'd said. But she'd already agreed to stay, wore his ring. To keep her dependent on him, then? Was that it? By his own admission he was ruthless, but to take her money and not tell her? Yet he had set a trap for her, hadn't he? Admitted he'd known where she was all those years. Had bided his time, calculated the odds and, the moment the time was right, had sprung the trap, when she was shocked, not thinking clearly.

How could she be in love with someone like that? How could he love her and do something like that? But he'd never said that he loved her, had he? her mind insisted—and she came to an abrupt halt. *Wanted*, he'd said. I've always wanted you. Not *loved*. Want my brand on you. A possession. Feeling slightly sick, she turned and gazed unseeingly back along the way she had come. Yet she had felt the same way in Rome—only not quite in the same way? Biting her lip hard, she slowly began to retrace her steps. She needed him to love her, not just want her. If he loved her, truly cared for her, and had taken the money in desperation, in a moment of madness, she'd be able to understand, forgive. But Foster didn't have moments of desperation, did he? He was always in control... Had it been that he needed the money? After all, she only had his word for it that he was a millionaire... So, if he didn't love her... Terrified of pursuing that line of thought, she quickened her pace. She had to know—one way or the other, she had to know.

Cutting through the woods, she brushed impatiently through the wet undergrowth, and, as she came out on to the path to the house, halted uncertainly. An elderly woman was leaning against the porch, head down as though needing to catch her breath. At Zoe's approach she looked warily up.

'Oh,' she exclaimed weakly, 'I thought you were David.'

'David?' she echoed blankly. 'Oh, Foster. He's inside, I think—I'll go and get him. Who shall I say is calling?'

After a small hesitation, the woman admitted, almost reluctantly, 'His mother.'

'His mother?' Zoe exclaimed in shock, her move to push the front door open halted. 'You're David's mother?'

'Yes.'

Staring at her, Zoe wondered almost hysterically how many more shocks she was likely to get that day. 'You'd better come in,' she mumbled awkwardly. It was hardly her place to question the woman, ask all the questions she'd like to know the answers to. Yet more questions without answers, she thought drearily.

'No. I'll wait here.'

With a helpless little shake of her head, Zoe went into the house to look for Foster. The house was empty. Perhaps he'd gone to look for her. Perhaps he hadn't. He could only be on foot, for his car was still parked outside. He'd also taken the Major. She retraced her steps to confront his mother. She felt exhausted and didn't honestly think she could take much more. 'He doesn't appear to be in,' she said. 'Do you want to wait? I don't suppose he'll be long.'

'No, I...' and to Zoe's horror, slow tears began to trickle down the lined face. 'I'm sorry,' apologised the woman awkwardly. 'If I could just wait here a moment, get my breath before I have to walk back to the bus stop... Maybe a drink of water...'

'Oh, for goodness' sake!' Zoe exclaimed. 'Whatever differences there are between you and your son, I'm sure he won't begrudge you a cup of tea and a sit down!'

'No, but I don't have long—before I have to get back, I mean. But, if he's not in, I'll have to come back later.' Looking worried and unsure, she turned as if to go.

'Have you been here before?' asked Zoe curiously.

'Yes, once,' she admitted, and Zoe frowned in confusion. When she'd asked if he knew where his parents were, he had said that he didn't know. 'I don't think he was very pleased to see me,' she continued quietly. 'Can't forgive me, I suppose. But I didn't give him away because I didn't love him,' she muttered brokenly. 'I did! But with no money, nowhere to live, his father off somewhere, I thought it would be best. He would be adopted, brought up in a good home...'

'Only it didn't work out like that,' Zoe murmured helplessly. She should have been appalled, compassionate, feel something, dammit! Only she didn't seem able to feel anything except irritation with this woman, and then was immediately ashamed. God knew her own troubles seemed minor by comparison. Looking at the woman properly for the first time, taking in the shabby coat, down-at-heel shoes, the sopping headscarf that covered her grey hair, Zoe gave a long sigh. The eyes were the same, she noted. Dark brown, like her son's. Unfathomable. 'Why did you come today?' she asked more gently.

'Because I was desperate,' admitted the woman tearfully, twisting the strap of her cheap bag round and round in her fingers.

'Desperate for what?' Zoe prompted.

'Money,' she whispered. 'I got into debt.'

'But surely the social services . . .'

'No. They already pay the rates and electricity, and I, well, I took out a loan . . .'

'And now you can't pay it back,' Zoe finished for her. My God, the times she'd heard that. It was so easy to borrow the money and because they were so desperate they didn't stop to think of the enormous payments they'd have to make to pay it back. The extortionate rate of interest. 'How much do you owe?'

'Four hundred pounds,' she admitted shamefaced. 'I'd pay it back, a bit each week. I've got a little cleaning job . . . It would just be a loan,' she murmured. 'I didn't know where else to turn . . .' They both swung round guiltily as they heard the dog bark. Foster was walking along the path, the dog bounding ahead of him. At his sharp command, the dog halted and sat. Foster's face was a cold mask, devoid of expression. He didn't look at Zoe, all his attention focused on his mother.

'David, I . . .' she began weakly.

'Go,' he said flatly, not allowing her to finish.

With a miserable little nod, she put her head down and began to shuffle down the path.

'Foster, you can't . . .'

'Be quiet,' he said coldly.

'Dammit, Foster! She's your mother!'

'I said be quiet,' he repeated with soft menace, and the dog gave a low growl.

'I heard what you said,' she gritted, her own temper beginning to simmer, 'but you can't let an old lady walk back to wherever she walked from! Foster!' she snapped when he ignored her. Her mouth tight, she turned on her heel and stormed into the house, grabbed her car keys and stormed back out again. Evading Foster's hand as he tried to stop her, she marched to her car, got in and turned on the engine with a furious twist of her hand. If he tried to stop her, she'd run him over! Over-revving the engine, she roared out of the drive. She didn't even glance at Foster. As she drew level with his mother, she screeched to a halt and flung open the passenger door. 'Get in,' she said peremptorily.

Foster's mother climbed meekly in, seemingly shaking. So was Zoe, but with temper. 'Where to?' she asked bluntly.

'If you could just drop me at the bus stop...'

'To where?'

'Brighton. But I can get the bus...'

Not bothering to answer, Zoe let out the clutch, and drove far too fast along the narrow lanes until she reached the main road. In truth she wasn't totally sure how to get to Brighton, but she had a vague recollection that Haywards Heath was in the right direction. Even if it wasn't, they'd get there eventually, and she was still in too much of a temper to care. Had she so misjudged him? she wondered. Wasn't he anything like the man she'd thought him? And how could he treat his mother so coldly, so nastily? Whatever the rights and wrongs, surely he had some compassion? Her lovely face set in a scowl, she ignored her passenger as her thoughts whirled unprofitably round and round. Halting at a junction and scanning the signpost, she turned right towards the coast and, she hoped, Brighton.

As they reached the outskirts of the town, Zoe broke the silence for the first time. 'You'll have to direct me,' she requested. 'I'm not very familiar with Brighton.'

'If you could just drop me off by the pier, I can walk from there,' Foster's mother said quietly.

'All right,' and, seeing a space, Zoe pulled in. Turning off the engine, she gave a long sigh before turning to face his mother. 'I'm sorry, I haven't been exactly sympathetic. I was just so angry...'

'It's all right. I shouldn't have gone. Only...'

'Yes. You were desperate... Perhaps when he's calmed down...'

'No. I don't think so. And you mustn't be angry with him—I can understand why he's like he is. So many years with nothing—I suppose that when you do get something, you hang on to it for all it's worth.'

Do you? Zoe wondered bleakly. Was that what it was all about? Retaining wealth?

Power? It was beginning to look very much like it. 'What will you do?' she asked.

'Oh, I'll manage, I expect,' the woman murmured, giving Zoe a sad smile. 'Perhaps I'll win the pools.'

Giving that piece of wishful thinking the derision it deserved, Zoe suggested, 'Perhaps if you wrote to him. Explained.'

'Perhaps. Anyway, it's not your worry. You've been very kind. Are you going to marry him? I see you're wearing an engagement ring.'

Staring down at it, Zoe was tempted, for just a moment, to give it to his mother, but then thought better of it. 'Yes, we're going to be married,' she admitted quietly. If we can sort out this muddle. 'I'll try and explain to him when I get back—perhaps he'll change his mind. Do you have a number I can contact you on? An address?'

'You could leave a message at the King's Hotel, for Mrs Lucan. I remarried,' she explained.

'All right.'

'Would you ... could you let me know one way or the other?' she asked hesitantly.

'Yes,' Zoe sighed. 'I'll ring tomorrow.'

As his mother climbed from the car, and carefully closed the door, Zoe gave her a limp wave, and then, with an illegal U-turn, drove back towards Petworth. Two miles from home she ran out of petrol, and, just to make the day perfect, it began to rain again. Fat heavy drops that plopped against the roof of the car, ran sluggishly down the windscreen. Feeling extraordinarily tired and depressed, she climbed out and turned her collar up. Locking the car door, she set off for home. She had no money on her, no umbrella, not even a scarf. And even if she'd had money there was no garage nearby. It was almost dark, and with evening it became colder as, wet and shivery, she trudged on, her hands in her pockets. Angry, hurt, bewildered, she didn't even bother to hurry. You could only get so wet.

Going into the house by the back door, ignoring the dog, who thumped his tail in greeting, she walked through and into the hall, and came face to face with Foster.

'Where the hell have you been?' he demanded angrily.

'You know where the hell I've been...'

'Not till this time! My God, Zoe, can't you think of anyone else but yourself?'

'Can't I what?' she asked in disbelief. 'Well, that really takes the biscuit, doesn't it? *I* didn't just turn my mother away!'

'No, *I* did! And for a very good reason, which you obviously have no desire to hear! And why the hell are you wet?'

'Because I ran out of bloody petrol!'

'Then I suggest you go and get out of those wet things before you get pneumonia. If you'll tell me where the car is...'

'To hell with the car,' she gritted. 'I have more important things on my mind, like, first, why you appropriated my money, and, second, why the hell you treat your mother as though she were a no-account tramp. I also want to know what the hell it *is* you feel for me, because it surely at the moment doesn't feel like being loved.'

'Go and get out of those wet things, then . . .'

'No!' she yelled. 'Now, Foster! I want to know now!'

Staring at her, he said softly, 'Don't dictate to me, Zoe. When you've changed, are calmer, we'll talk.' Then he deliberately turned his back, and walked into the study, closing the door between them. With a little growl of temper, she flung the door open so that it crashed against the wall.

'Don't you ever shut a door in my face!' she yelled, incensed. 'You may think that you can ride roughshod over everybody, make up your own rules, but let me tell you, David Campbell, that I am neither an elderly mother, nor a managing director who can be fired with impunity. Granted I owe you for taking me in when I was homeless. Granted you have to date treated me with courtesy and consideration. Granted I have no right to interfere over the way you treat your mother, but I *do* have the right to know why you took the insurance money, and I *do* have the right to know how you really feel about me!'

'Yes, you do—and you're going exactly the right way to ensure that I explain nothing,' he said coldly, his own mouth a tight, clamped line. 'Stop being melodramatic...'

'Oh, melodramatic, is it?' she gritted sarcastically.

'Yes. And let me make one thing very clear to you, Zoe. Just because I care for you does not mean that I will explain my every action, and the way I treat my employees and my mother is no concern of yours...'

'Not even if she's in danger of being imprisoned for debt?' she exaggerated.

'Not even then. My mother is not what she seems—and if she's been asking for money, I will inform you here and now that she will not get it. Not from me. Not from you. I've put a stop on the facility you have to draw funds from my account. And, for your information, I did not misappropriate your money!' Walking over to his desk, he yanked open the drawer and withdrew an unopened envelope, tossing it on the desk between them. 'I merely...'

'Merely kept it from me! Which is theft.'

'Which is putting it in safe keeping, and then forgetting to give it to you.'

'Don't talk such utter rubbish!' she exploded. 'You deliberately kept it from me! And Mr McKinley said he rang you to say it was coming...'

'You were out at the time, and I forgot to tell you...'

'You bastard!'

'Quite possibly,' he agreed with a nasty little sneer. Leaning his hips back against the desk and folding his arms across his chest, he asked, with every appearance of interest, 'How much was she asking for, by the way?'

'Four hundred,' gritted Zoe.

'Restrained of her,' he said with a nasty sneer. 'Perhaps she's learning. The last time it was a thousand.'

'I don't care about the last time. I care about now!' Staring at him, her eyes hard, she said unevenly, 'Did you really think I wouldn't find out? Or that I would meekly accept it when I did? I once told you not to expect me meekly to agree to your dictates. Didn't I? I begin to think now that the shock of the fire, the pleasure of seeing you again, addled my brain. I foolishly thought you respected me as a person—I thought, hoped you saw me as an equal, but you don't, do you? I'm not a toy, Foster, someone to pat on the head from time to time. Marriage is a partnership, give and take, on both sides. You seem to expect that I will give all you want to take. Well, I won't, I need more than that.' Taking off her ring, she put it on the desk. 'I don't think I want to be married to someone who cares for me so little.'

Her vision blurred by tears, she picked up the envelope and turned quickly away. She heard him call her name, but was too angry, too hurt, to respond; she just needed to escape. Ignoring him, she walked out, and closed the door quietly.

In her own room she threw herself across the bed. She didn't think that she'd ever felt so hurt or miserable in her whole life. Rolling over on to her back, she stared at the ceiling. There was a hard, tight pain in her chest, an ache in her lungs. Well, she'd wondered how he would treat her when he was in a temper, and now she knew. Maybe they'd both been too long on their own. Had both grown too used to being selfish. She'd also known that to demand answers was not the best way of handling him— but he hadn't denied not loving her, had he? Perhaps a few days away on her own would make things clearer. Perhaps.

Determinedly shutting her mind to everything that had happened, she got swiftly to her feet. Cramming underwear and a change of jeans and sweater into a plastic carrier, she picked up her bag. As she checked that she had her replacement credit cards and some money, she glanced at the letter, and saw the insurance company logo across the front. So that was how he'd known it was from the insurance company. Shoving it into her bag, she went quietly downstairs and out through the back door. At the end of the lane she called a cab from the phonebox. Although she had only a few minutes to wait, she was on tenterhooks in case Foster should have discovered she'd gone, and come after her. Although why he should she didn't know. He'd been as angry as herself... When the cab arrived, she climbed thankfully into the back. Quietly explaining her need for petrol, and to get her car started, she sank back and stared blindly through the rain-lashed window.

She booked into the Norfolk Hotel in Brighton, for the simple reason that it had a car park at the front and she wouldn't have to spend ages looking for somewhere to put the car. They gave her a room in the annexe, which meant a five-hundred-mile walk up and down little corridors. Once in her room, she closed and locked the door and gave in to her misery. Running away never solved anything, yet she needed a few days on her own to think things out, try to understand her feelings. They would have to talk eventually, for she knew herself well enough to realise that she would need an explanation from him, even if it wasn't what she wanted to know. She shouldn't have lost her temper. Should have let him explain then. Rolling on to her side, she closed her eyes and allowed the tears that she had been holding in check to fall unheeded.

The next few days she spent wandering round Brighton. She'd made no decisions about her future, about what she should do next—it was almost as though she were back in limbo, the way she'd been after the fire. She ate out mostly, when she remembered, and at lunchtime of the third day, unable to face her room again, unable to face food, she went into the American Bar at the hotel and ordered a large gin and tonic. In truth, she was missing him more than she'd thought possible. Had thought, stupidly, that it would be easy to go back to being on her own. She hadn't really missed Peter when they'd broken up. All she could see was Foster's face as she had last seen it. Hard, cold, the eyes empty.

Seating herself at a table in the corner by the windows, she stared out at the people wandering along the front, and then suddenly, out of the conversations ranging around her, one word stood out. King's. King's Hotel, she remembered, and realised guiltily that she hadn't left a message for Foster's mother. In her own misery she'd completely forgotten hers. When she'd finished her drink, she decided, she'd go and phone. Presumably Reception could give her the number.

But once outside influences had intruded into her thoughts, she found herself idly listening to the snippets of conversation, and she gave a small, humourless smile. People with busy lives, all going about their own concerns, with their own worries, cares, uppermost. Just like herself.

As she got to her feet to leave, a woman's shrill laugh made her halt and turn her head— and her eyes locked with those of Foster's mother. Not the downtrodden woman she had seen before, but a well-dressed, heavily made-up woman whose brown eyes—Foster's eyes— stared back at her in horrified fascination. Not what she seems, Foster had said. With a rather cynical little smile pulling at her mouth, Zoe made her way across to the woman's table. The grey hair that Zoe had seen beneath the head-scarf was highlighted with blonde streaks. Expensive, flashy rings decorated the thin hands, the nails painted a bright, glowing red to match her lipstick.

'Hello, Mrs Lucan,' she said quietly. 'Your fortunes seem to have taken a turn for the better. Win the pools, did you?' Without waiting for a reply, she turned and walked out. At the desk, she asked for her bill to be made ready, then quickly went to her room to collect her belongings. Not that it really made any difference to the fact that Foster should have explained—or could have explained—but wandering round Brighton, being thoroughly miserable, seemed exceedingly stupid. And if he hadn't missed her? Had discovered that he didn't want her, after all?

The drive to the house seemed to take forever, yet in reality it took only twenty minutes. Parking in the drive, next to Foster's car, she hurried inside. The house had an empty feel, yet if his car was there he couldn't be far. And where was Laura? Pushing into the kitchen, finding it empty, she dropped her bag on the table, and went out and swiftly upstairs. No one. Perhaps he'd taken the Major for a walk. No way could she sit around waiting for him to come back—having taken the decision to return, she needed to see him now.

Hurrying back downstairs, she went out of the back door. Listening intently for sounds of the dog, and hearing none, she walked in the direction he usually took, pushing impatiently into the wet and dripping woods. After half an hour of desperate searching, calling his name, she turned, and began walking disconsolately back to the house—and that was when she saw him. He didn't look exactly ecstatic, either. Her legs weak, she leaned against a nearby tree.

It seemed like forever since she'd seen him, and, if she'd had any doubts before about how she felt, she had none now. She loved him. Needed him. Needed to see his odd smile. Needed the warmth of his body next to hers. He wouldn't change—he'd told her he wouldn't. But could she live with never knowing how he thought or felt? Could she live without him? Well, she could, of course she could, but she doubted that it would be a very fulfilled existence. He gave her challenges that stretched her mind. Her perceptions. He had more confidence in her than she had in herself, made her a fuller person . . . and she wanted to touch him. Hold him. Feel his mouth teasing her own. He never rushed, hurried, their love-making was always slow, leisurely, and her stomach cramped in sudden memory of the sheer mind-blowing excitement of it. Of his lazy smile, of his crazy innovations—and his manipulation, she added honestly. Because he was a manipulator.

He also looked incredibly lonely, standing there watching the dog ferret in the under-growth. His hands were thrust deep into his jacket pockets, his dark hair fell damply across his forehead, and she wanted to touch it, brush it back. His strong face seemed brooding, vulnerable—and, for a second, he was the fifteen-year-old boy she had adored.

CHAPTER EIGHT

'OH, FOSTER.'

The dog saw her first, and came bounding over, his tail going like a metronome, and she bent to hug him, fondle his ears, to give herself time. Looking up, she slowly straightened. His eyes were empty, she saw, and she suddenly realised something that she should perhaps have appreciated a long time ago. It wasn't the blankness of indifference in his eyes, but the emptiness of being alone. Had this man never been loved? Had no one ever given him a hug just because? Not for his wealth, or his attraction, but because he was simply himself?

He didn't hurry towards her, but then she'd never expected that he would; he just walked quietly to stand in front of her. Looked at her, and her heart turned painfully over.

'Hello,' she whispered, her voice a mere thread of sound. 'I'm sorry.'

'I think that's my line,' he murmured, his eyes bleak.

'No,' she said gently. 'It doesn't matter whose fault it was, a bit of both, I expect... I was angry, hurt and bewildered.'

'Yes. Wilful,' and his voice sounded so empty, so defeated.

'I lost my temper. I needed time to think, sort myself out.'

'And did you?'

'Yes. I missed you. More than I would have believed possible.'

'Yes.' And just that one word meant more to her than the most flowery of declarations, because she knew that he meant that he had missed her, too. Taking one hand from his pocket, a hand that trembled, he gently pushed the tumbled hair off her face. 'It felt as though you had died . . . No,' he exclaimed, as her eyes filled with tears, 'don't cry. I think that would destroy me utterly.' Taking a deep, heavy breath, he continued in the same soft, slightly thick voice, 'Wanting to kiss you, hold you, make love to you, has been a torture of the worst kind.'

'Oh, Foster,' she said brokenly, one hand going out to him, and, as though that were more than he could possibly bear, he suddenly pulled her violently into his arms, crushed her impossibly tight.

'Oh, Tiger,' he muttered. 'Sometimes I've felt I've lived on the loneliest place on earth, but these last few days have been a nightmare of grief, a glimpse of eternal hell. How could you think I didn't love you? How could you think my feelings for you weren't deep?' Wrenching her back, he stared down into her face. 'Don't you have any idea how you make me feel?'

'You only said want...' she began weakly, her voice shaking.

'Yes. I didn't know the words, I didn't know if they meant what I felt. And, even if I had, I didn't know how to say them. It seemed such an impossible dream. But you should have known, Zoe,' he added helplessly. 'You should have known.' His hands gripping her shoulders hard, he took a shuddering breath before continuing, 'It wasn't waiting for the right opportunity that made me hesitate to get in touch with you once you had grown up, seen how beautiful you were...'

'Seen?' she asked softly.

'Yes,' he admitted with a crooked smile. 'Like a love-lorn swain, haunting your haunts...'

'Haunting? Now, that I don't believe.'

'Well, all right, maybe not haunting,' he qualified. 'I came back, you know, when you were sixteen, waited outside the school for you to come out. I was going to give you the money then, ask if you remembered me...'

'Why didn't you?'

'Because you weren't alone. You had a crowd of boys round you, vying for your attention—and I didn't want to share you. Even in your school uniform you were beautiful—flaunting it,' he added with a small smile, and when she scowled he hugged her to him again, his mouth briefly touching her neck. With a determined effort, he stood back. 'If I touch you now, kiss you as I want to, I won't be able to stop... So

I went away. I would wait until you grew up, I decided. Whenever I was in town, or—um—Berkshire, strictly on business, you understand, I would check on you, make sure you were all right.'

'Oh, Foster, I would have been so pleased to have seen you. For weeks, months after you left, I used to watch for you. So sure you would come back—only you never did. I imagined all sorts of horrors. You'd been arrested, sent away, locked up. I was so afraid for you, and I couldn't ask anybody...' Giving a big sigh, she smiled at him. 'There was the most awful fuss, police...'

'Police?' he asked in astonishment.

'Oh, yes. You'd disappeared, no one knew where—you surely didn't expect that no one would look for you? Fostered children aren't allowed to go missing, you know. There are social workers, the people from the orphanage, police. Not that I really understood then what was going on, just aware of the fuss, grown-ups muttering. I was terrified the police were going to question me—only they didn't. Thought I was too young to understand, I expect.'

'I'm sorry. I have to confess, I didn't even think about the stink I might have left behind. Did they think that I'd been murdered?'

'Oh, no. People who've been murdered don't pack their clothes. No, they had to follow it up because you were a minor, I suppose—and it doesn't look too good for the authorities when a child runs away from foster-parents that they've designated ... You didn't even write to me,' she murmured, remembering how tragic she'd felt. A plump little girl watching for the post, watching for the boy who never came. 'Why didn't you?'

'I don't know. I think I thought you were too young to read properly. I don't know,' he repeated, giving her a faint smile.

'But you could have come, later, when the fuss had died down. Come to see me. Why didn't you?' she asked softly.

'Cowardice, I suspect. You were beautiful and talented ...'

'But you're the most confident person I know. You never seem to have self-doubts.'

'Don't I?'

'Do you?' she asked dubiously.

'Of course I do, you silly girl. Oh, I kept telling myself the time wasn't right, to wait, but I think it was probably more the vague idea that, if I didn't contact you, I could pretend that one day it would all come right. Taking risks is fine if you aren't terribly bothered about the outcome, but the outcome of *that* was too important to take a chance on its all going wrong ... I'd never felt like that before, never wanted someone as I wanted you, and I think maybe I was a bit ashamed of the intensity of my feelings. Emotional outpourings were frowned upon where I grew up, and probably I let things get a little bit out of proportion, whatever ... And then, after the fire, when you came to stay, I knew that I could never let you go. I needed you. So, like you with your plants, I was careful—restrained—and, bit by bit, I began to believe you might come to care for me. But I kept remembering how you wanted to be independent, even after you agreed to marry me, and I was afraid to take the chance that you would leave. So, when the insurance money came through—I kept it from you. I had tried, I suppose, to make you dependent on me, but once you had the money you would no longer need me, and I was afraid that our relationship might disintegrate into dust. When you build on shaky foundations, you can't expect the structure to stand. So I lied, by omission.'

'You didn't need the money?'

'No, of course I didn't need the money. I was just so terrified that, once you realised you could be independent, you'd leave.'

'But I loved you . . .' she said helplessly.

'Did you? I don't think I quite believed that. Not sure I do now.'

'Oh, darling. I do, I think I only realised how much when I was away from you. I'm afraid it was a bit like a child shouting defiantly in the dark.'

'Sort of "you'll be sorry when I've gone"?'

'Yes,' she agreed, with a small laugh. 'I can remember saying that to my father when he'd told me off over something. "I'm going to run away, and if I get run over *then* you'll be sorry." Emotional blackmail—only I don't think I intended it to be that. I just felt so confused. Like you, I'd never been in love before. It makes a muck of rationality, doesn't it?'

'Yes. But then I don't think I've ever been rational where you're concerned... I couldn't believe you'd gone. After you stormed out of the study, I left it a little while before following you, to marshal my explanation, give you time to calm down. I went up to your room, and you'd gone. I think part of me died forever in that moment. I couldn't believe I'd been such a fool. I couldn't believe I'd lost you.'

'Just temporarily mislaid,' she said softly, her fingers gentle at his nape, soothing, touching, warming, needing to feel his warmth. 'And I'm not altogether sure I believe your version.' She smiled. 'Doesn't sound much like the man I've come to know.'

'Doesn't it? Then perhaps I'd better just let you keep your illusions about me,' he murmured, with another of his endearing smiles. 'But, for all those years, you were my reason for being, my yardstick. My dream.' Framing her face with warm palms, he continued, 'I'm not proud of what I did, although I have to confess that the shame's more because I was found out. But, if I tell you that I'll never do anything like it again, will you believe me?'

'Yes,' she said simply.

'Yes? Just like that? You make it hard for a man, Zoe. Your simple belief makes it imperative not to fail—and that's not easy.'

'But entirely possible,' she smiled. 'I should have believed you about your mother. Should have known you'd have a reason for your behaviour. I wasn't seeing very clearly. I'm sorry.'

'We neither of us were, but I should have explained. She turned up the first time two years ago, just after I'd moved in here. God knows how she found me. I was quite prepared to meet her half-way—until she started on her explanation, her tale of poverty. It never quite rang true. So I had someone watch her—and of course it wasn't true. She was a confidence trickster. Money by deception. She conned the social services, landlords, heaven knows who else. She and her boyfriend, Lucan, live by their wits.'

'She's not married to him?'

'No. She couldn't claim half the benefits she does if she were married to him. He'd be a visible means of support. No, they have separate flats—and claim independently.'

'And then she made the mistake of trying to con *you.*'

'Yes. When she returned, she asked for a thousand. I told her never to come back.'

'Yes, I can imagine,' she smiled. She doubted that he'd said anything so simple as 'Don't come back.' 'And you couldn't tell me?' she asked softly.

'No. It wasn't easy to admit my shame.'

'Shame?' she asked, astonished. 'For what do you have to feel ashamed?'

'Whatever the rights and wrongs of it, she gave me birth. I carry her genes. It's not easy living with the knowledge that your mother is a confidence trickster. Do you think I don't wonder sometimes if that isn't why I made money so easily? Because of an inherited skill?'

'Oh, darling, don't be a fool. You have too much pride not to deal honestly...'

'I didn't deal very honestly with you.'

'No, but that was a bit different, wasn't it? I bet you can't name me one other whom you've deliberately deceived in order to make a profit.'

When he remained silent, she gave a small triumphant smile. 'But I still don't really understand why she came. If you'd already made it abundantly clear that you would have nothing further to do with her, why did she come? What did she hope to gain?'

'Because, I imagine, she'd heard that I'd got engaged, probably waited until she saw me go out, thought you might be an easy touch.'

'But she couldn't have known—you wouldn't have told me about her—or, yes, I suppose she could. If she knew enough about you, she'd have known that you never tell anyone anything,' she said wryly.

'Mm. But I suspect that she hoped you'd give her some money before I returned—only I came back too soon.'

'Maybe. I saw her in Brighton ... I hope that I don't have to see her again.' For a moment Zoe's face was hard. Then, touching his cheek gently, moving her fingers slowly across his still taut face, she added quietly, 'Take me home.'

'To stay?'

'To stay,' she confirmed huskily.

With his funny half-smile, he held out his hand and she grasped it warmly. 'I like to have my hand held, remember?'

'Yes, I remember,' she said softly.

They walked back to the house in silence. Without breaking their hold, they went up-stairs and into his room. Warmth and ex-citement were coursing through her as he let go of her hand. Her throat was dry, her heart beating over-fast, as they faced each other. Slipping out of her jacket, she let it fall to the floor and deliberately began to strip. His face a still, controlled mask, the only sign of emotion a small nerve jumping in his jaw, he followed suit. Moving to the wide bed, one each side, their eyes remained locked and Zoe felt suddenly light-headed. Kneeling slowly on the edge of the bed, she gradually lay down, and waited for Foster to do the same. The clouds, parting momentarily, sent a shaft of weak sun-light across her, shadowing Foster, hiding his expression, but there was no hiding the arousal of his body, nor the hard peaks of her breasts. He was shaking as he lay face-down beside her, his forearms supporting his weight, his eyes never leaving hers. Slowly, he rolled on to his side and scooped her to rest against him.

'Hold me tight,' he instructed shakily. 'Ankle to ankle, knee to knee, thigh to thigh.'

With a little groan, she fitted herself to him, two halves of a whole finally joined. Lying quietly for long, long moments, warmth from each other spread, relaxed tense muscles, and, stretching her neck upwards, she placed a soft butterfly kiss on his chin, his jaw, his nose and finally his mouth, and slowly closed her eyes. 'Make love to me,' she whispered. 'Touch me, hold me, feel me, hurt me even, but make it real, Foster, and whatever stupid things I might say in the future, ignore them, don't take away the feel of you.'

'No...no,' and the long shaky sigh he gave transmitted itself to her.

'Love me.'

'Yes.' Then, with a funny little laugh, he murmured softly, 'It will have to be slow the next time—right at this moment being slow, leisurely, would kill me.'

Moving swiftly, he covered her body with his and his mouth descended to hers, parted it, as her thighs parted for him.

As they lay clasped tightly in each other's arms, as their breathing slowly returned to normal, she whispered, 'I think I ended up with the wrong name. Tiger should more rightly belong to you.'

'Did I hurt you?' he asked softly, contritely, his breathing still slightly fast.

'No... Oh, Foster,' she exclaimed, rolling away and spreading her arms wide, her body revelling in the warm ache, the stretched muscles. 'I love you. I think I'm going to be insatiable.'

'Promise?' he asked softly, leaning up so that he could watch her.

'Mm. Promise.' Opening her eyes, she gave him a wide, happy grin. 'I feel as though I've been away for ever—and now I've come home.'

'Yes. You will stay?'

'Yes.' Staring at him, at the strong face that seemed so sombre, so still, her heart began to race again—in excitement, in pleasure, in gratitude. This quiet, deep man, was hers. Part of her past, part of her future, and if she ever lost him she thought that she would die.

'I love you,' she said softly, reaching out to touch him. To trace her fingers along his strong jaw, his mouth, then up into the thick hair that was so liberally sprinkled with grey. Drawing his head down, she touched her mouth to his. Then touched again as she felt him shiver. Moved her thigh between his, revelled in the warmth of firm skin against hers, the taste of him. 'Oh, Foster, you do love me?'

'Yes,' he said thickly. 'Dear God, *yes*.' Rolling her over on to her back, he covered her mouth with his, deepening the kiss almost violently, his arms steel bands about her slim frame. 'I want you with me forever. I don't want to let you out of my sight. Don't want any other man to ever look at you. I don't think you have any idea how desperately hard I fought to appear indifferent.' Then, giving a small crooked smile, he added, 'That night in the sitting-room, when I first kissed you, and you said it didn't affect me—remember?'

'Yes,' she agreed softly, remembering it very well. She had been unable to forget how he had made her feel.

'I wanted to take you there, on the sofa, on the floor, and if you hadn't gone to bed when you did I would have had to, before I lost control.' His eyes deep and dark, holding hers, he added softly, 'I want to lose control now.' Then, his eyes closing briefly, his voice thickening, he gasped, 'There are so many things I want to do to you, for you, with you . . .'

'Then do them,' she said shakily.

'No,' he said hoarsely, 'later.' Taking a deep shuddering breath, he rolled on to his back, and put his arm over his eyes. 'Later.'

'Coward,' she taunted, rolling to lie with her arms across his chest. Gently removing his arm, she stared into his face until he opened his eyes.

'Where you're concerned I'm the biggest coward alive. I'm so terrified of losing you.'

'You won't,' she reassured him.

'No. Why can't I believe it? Oh, Zoe, Zoe, you drive a man insane.' Summoning up a lop-sided smile, he added, 'I don't know that I'm the best candidate for a husband, but I will try to be—more outgoing. I'm not sure I can change—I was programmed too young, and after thirty-four years of keeping my own counsel, hiding my feelings, the mould is too inflexible. But whatever I do, however impossible you may find me, will you remember that

I do love you? That you're my reason for living? Working? Breathing? Will you remember that, Zoe?'

'Yes,' she said huskily.

Planting a swift kiss on her nose, he slowly ran a finger down her spine. 'I measured all other women by you. By my memories of you. They had to be loyal, tough, fighters. They had to be warm, compassionate, self-contained—why are you smiling?'

'Because I measured all men by you,' she admitted softly.

'Kismet?'

'Maybe. Or just two people who were too impressionable for their own good. Two people with a dream that wouldn't die.'

'Yes, a dream that wouldn't die. You were the only person who ever defended me. Without knowing the facts, the reasons behind my behaviour, a tiger with one very large cub. Unqualified championship—I always tried to live up to that,' he murmured, 'your seven-year-old belief in me.'

'Did you always succeed?'

'No,' he laughed. Taking her hand, he held it to his mouth and gently kissed each finger.

'I didn't do so well on the unqualified championship lately, did I?' she asked ruefully. 'In fact, I was a miserable failure.'

'Not miserable, never miserable—wholly delightful—and I'm finding it hard to believe that you're back, in my bed, lying on top of me—that I'm not dreaming.'

'You aren't dreaming,' she said firmly, then for good measure pinched him.

'Ouch.'

'Don't be a baby, didn't hurt you one little bit... Can I have my ring back, please?'

'Now? This minute?' he asked softly. 'Or will it wait until I've made love to you again?'

'It will wait,' she said happily. 'Foster?'

'Mm?'

'Do you want a family?'

'Oh, Zoe,' he sighed helplessly. 'I can only just cope with knowing that you're here, that you've come back. I drove around for three days searching for you, asking strangers if they'd seen you, ringing hotels within a twenty-mile radius, despairing... A family? Children? A future? Dear God, am I allowed so much?'

'Yes,' she said gently, 'and I suddenly find that I want to have your babies. One of each. A little boy that I can love, make up for all the horrors you endured. A little girl that will twist you round her little finger.'

'Like you, in fact,' he said drily.

'Me? Huh, some chance I have against you and your machinations. But not yet, eh? I'd like you to myself for a year or two first. To be selfish, to make love to you as and when we feel like it.'

'Like now?'

'Like now,' she confirmed.

Sliding his hand through her dark, tumbled hair, he drew her mouth to his. There was a fierce longing in his touch and her body melted.

Pushing her knee between his strong thighs, she felt his warmth and hardness and her groan of desire was echoed by his.

They were married two weeks later, by licence, at the little nearby church. Flying in the face of convention, they went to the ceremony together in Foster's car. Standing in the porch, Foster turned to her. Taking her hands in his, he asked quietly, 'All right?'

'Yes.' Squeezing his hands tightly together, she held them briefly against her breast. 'You're shaking,' she exclaimed softly. 'Are you nervous?'

'Not of being married, no, only of something preventing it.'

'Nothing will prevent it,' she comforted. With a warm smile she stood on tiptoe and kissed him. 'Come on.'

Walking hand in hand down the aisle, their footsteps echoing in the almost empty church, Zoe smiled at Laura who sat, with an elderly friend to serve as second witness, in the front pew.

Zoe tried to hold the simple ceremony in her mind, to absorb the atmosphere, the quiet rightness of it, so that she would remember every detail for all time. But the words, their meaning, spoken in the vicar's beautiful soft voice, held her instead. The warmth of Foster at her side, the specialness of the occasion, the sun that peeped shyly through the stained-glass window to throw a prism of colour across the altar, diverted her, uplifted her almost. She wasn't especially religious, but being married in God's house was right. It was what she had wanted, and Foster had made no objection. Despite the lack of wedding dress, brides- maids, or family, it was still a special day for her, and she had rung her mother the previous evening. They'd spent a long time talking, had promised she and Foster would both visit the States as soon as possible.

In something of a daze, a beautiful dream almost, she made her responses, and, as Foster slipped the ring on her finger, her vision blurred for a moment, and then she looked up at him and gave him a tremulous smile. 'For better or worse,' she murmured softly for his ears alone.

'Yes,' he agreed, equally softly.

They knelt together, for the prayer and dec- laration of marriage.

'You may kiss the bride,' the vicar said.

'Pleasure,' Foster murmured, with his fas- cinating half-smile, and she gave a soft laugh and raised her face for his kiss.

As soon as the formalities were completed, and she'd signed her name in the register, they walked outside and both paused on the steps and looked out at the world, almost as if expecting it to look different. Turning to look at each other, they smiled, then laughed as Laura rushed in front of them, camera poised. Straightening the jacket of her cream wool suit and making sure that her buttonhole hadn't wilted, Zoe beamed proudly into the camera, her hand tucked into the crook of Foster's arm.

'Thanks, Laura,' Foster said easily, then, taking both women by surprise, bent and kissed Laura's cheek. 'I'll bring the Major over later this evening—sure you don't mind having him?'

'Of course not, he'll be good company. The cats might not be so fond of the idea, but I am. Now, you're not to worry about anything. I'll keep an eye on the house, and take very good care of the dog. Now go on, off you both go.'

As they walked hand in hand back to his car, Zoe stared unashamedly at her new husband. Mine, she thought. This distinguished-looking man is mine. In his dark three-piece suit, the red rose in his buttonhole, he looked— magnificent. Delaying him for a moment as he bent to unlock the car door, she stared deep into the dark brown eyes that held a faint smile.

'I love you,' she said softly. 'Very much.'

'And I you,' he assured her, 'more than very much. More than life itself.' Then, with a small smile, he admitted, 'I feel shell-shocked—and I want to make love to my wife. I want to undo that ridiculous topknot and tangle your hair the way I like it. I want to remove that smart suit that makes you look terrifyingly severe— and I want to hold you, and never let you go. So will you please get in the car, Mrs Campbell, so that I can take you back to the house and then, when I've satisfied my lust ...'

'Our mutual lust,' she corrected.

'Mutual lust,' he confirmed, with a little dip of his head. 'Then we shall fly to a remote island in the Pacific, where I can make love to you all day and every day—all night and every night until we're exhausted—and then we'll spend the rest of our lives thinking up new ways to please each other... Yes?'

'Yes—oh, yes—and will you do to me all the things you wouldn't do before?'

'Oh, yes,' he murmured, a smile in his eyes. 'Now that I have you bound to me, then yes, now I can lose control.'

'Oh, goody,' she said softly.

'I hope so,' he said, equally softly.

You'll flip . . . your pages won't!
Read paperbacks *hands-free* with

Book Mate · I

The perfect "mate" for all your romance paperbacks

Traveling • Vacationing • At Work • In Bed • Studying • Cooking • Eating

Perfect size for all standard paperbacks, this wonderful invention makes reading a pure pleasure! Ingenious design holds paperback books OPEN and FLAT so even wind can't ruffle pages — leaves your hands free to do other things. Reinforced, wipe-clean vinyl-covered holder flexes to let you turn pages without undoing the strap . . . supports paperbacks so well, they have the strength of hardcovers!

Pages turn WITHOUT opening the strap

SEE-THROUGH STRAP

Reinforced back stays flat.

Built in bookmark

BOOK MARK

BACK COVER HOLDING STRIP

10" x 7¼" opened.
Snaps closed for easy carrying, too

They went in through the terrace door. The house was dark, most of the servants were down at the circus, and only Nelbert's hired security guards were in sight. It was child's play for Blackheart to move past them, the work of two seconds to go through the solid lock on the terrace door. And then they were creeping through the darkened house, up the long curving stairs, Ferris fully as noiseless as the more experienced Blackheart.

They stopped on the second floor landing. "What if they have guns?" Ferris mouthed silently.

Blackheart shrugged. "Then duck."

"How reassuring," she responded. Footsteps directly above them signaled that the thieves were on the move, and so should they be.

For more romance, suspense and adventure, read Harlequin Intrigue. Two exciting titles each month, available wherever Harlequin Books are sold.

COMING IN 1991 FROM
HARLEQUIN SUPERROMANCE:

Three abandoned orphans,
one missing heiress!

Dying millionaire Owen Byrnside receives an
anonymous letter informing him that twenty-six years
ago, his son, Christopher, fathered a daughter. The
infant was abandoned at a foundling home that
subsequently burned to the ground, destroying all
records. Three young women could be Owen's long-
lost granddaughter, and Owen is determined to track
down each of them! Read their stories in

#434 HIGH STAKES (available January 1991)
#438 DARK WATERS (available February 1991)
#442 BRIGHT SECRETS (available March 1991)

Three exciting stories of intrigue and romance by
veteran Superromance author Jane Silverwood.